BEYOND THE RIVER

Books by Robert Elmer

ADVENTURES DOWN UNDER

#1 / *Escape to Murray River*
#2 / *Captive at Kangaroo Springs*
#3 / *Rescue at Boomerang Bend*
#4 / *Dingo Creek Challenge*
#5 / *Race to Wallaby Bay*
#6 / *Firestorm at Kookaburra Station*
#7 / *Koala Beach Outbreak*
#8 / *Panic at Emu Flat*

THE YOUNG UNDERGROUND

#1 / *A Way Through the Sea*
#2 / *Beyond the River*
#3 / *Into the Flames*
#4 / *Far From the Storm*
#5 / *Chasing the Wind*
#6 / *A Light in the Castle*
#7 / *Follow the Star*
#8 / *Touch the Sky*

PROMISE OF ZION

#1 / *Promise Breaker*
#2 / *Peace Rebel*

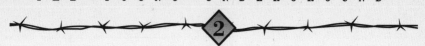
BEYOND THE RIVER

Robert Elmer

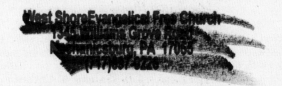

BETHANY HOUSE PUBLISHERS
MINNEAPOLIS, MINNESOTA 55438

Beyond the River
Copyright © 1994
Robert Elmer

Cover illustration by Chris Ellison

Published by Bethany House Publishers
A Ministry of Bethany Fellowship International
11400 Hampshire Avenue South
Minneapolis, Minnesota 55438
www.bethanyhouse.com

Printed in the United States of America by
Bethany Press International, Minneapolis, Minnesota 55438

Library of Congress Cataloging-in-Publication Data

Elmer, Robert.
    Beyond the river / Robert Elmer.
        p.   cm. — (The Young Underground ; #2)
    Summary: While visiting their cousins' farm on the west coast of Denmark in the summer of 1944, eleven-year-old twins Peter and Elise learn the power of prayer as they work to rescue a downed British pilot.

    1. World War, 1939–1945—Underground movements—Denmark—Juvenile fiction. [1. World War, 1939–1945—Underground movements—Denmark—Fiction. 2. Denmark—History—German occupation, 1940–1945—Fiction. 3. Brothers and sisters—Fiction. 4. Christian life—Fiction.] I. Title. II. Series: Elmer, Robert. Young underground ; #2.
PZ7.E4794Be   1994
[Fic]—dc20   94–19910
ISBN 1–55661–375–X   CIP
                                                                          AC

For my Danish parents,
who taught me never
to forget where we came from.

ROBERT ELMER has written and edited numerous articles for both newspapers and magazines in the Pacific Northwest. The *Young Underground* series was inspired by stories from Robert's Denmark-born parents, as well as friends who lived through the years of German occupation. He is currently a writer for the Raymond Group, a Christian advertising agency located near Seattle. He and his wife, Ronda, have three children and make their home in Poulsbo, Washington.

CONTENTS

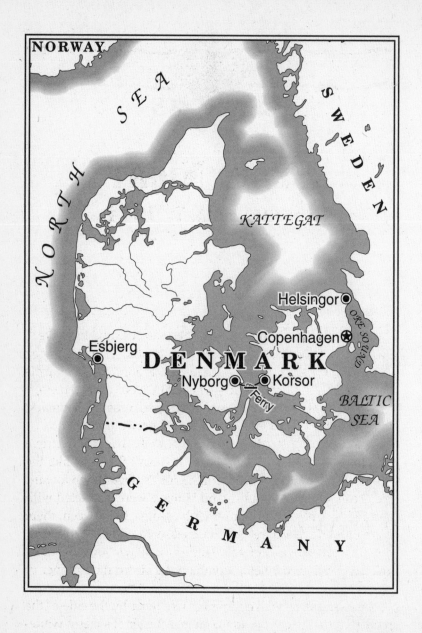

NORWAY

NORTH SEA

SWEDEN

KATTEGAT

Helsingor

ORE SOUND

Copenhagen

Esbjerg

DENMARK

Nyborg   Korsor

Ferry

BALTIC SEA

GERMANY

LIGHT NIGHT
FRIDAY, JULY 7, 1944

"So is this what you thought a sheep farm would look like?" Elise asked her eleven-year-old twin brother, Peter, as they stepped out of the little bus. She twirled around with her arms out, taking in the farm country where they would spend the rest of their summer vacation. This was the west coast of Denmark, the part of the country their mother had grown up in.

They set their bags down and waved at the driver as he drove slowly on down the country road. It wasn't flat here, like the rest of their country. Instead, rolling hills spilled down toward the ocean. The little mounds and hollows were blanketed with a shaggy purple carpet of heather blossoms. In between, there were pine and beech tree woods, checkered with fenced meadows full of sheep. An air force of little forktail swallows swooped and dipped over the fields, combing the air for their dinner of bugs.

Peter and Elise walked up to a wire fence by the side of the road and tried to get the attention of a cluster of shaggy, white-

faced sheep, but the animals barely looked up from their grazing.

"Yeah, this is what I thought it would look like," he finally
answered his sister. "Like in the picture books. This is going to
be great."

Elise propped her bony elbows on a fence post and gazed
out over the fields. Like her brother, she had golden blond hair
(only hers was down to her shoulders) and their father's steely
blue eyes. But she was quite a bit taller than Peter. He had long
since given up trying to stand on his tiptoes at the family growth
chart back home.

"Hallo!" came a voice from behind them.

Peter immediately recognized it as his Uncle Harald
Ringsted, his mother's sister's husband. They had only met him
once—before the war—and Peter could hardly remember that.
But the deep voice he *did* remember. Big and friendly.

Peter and Elise turned around to see their Uncle Harald trotting down the long gravel driveway of the sheep farm.

"Hi, Uncle Harald," said Elise shyly.

"Looks like you made it just fine." Uncle Harald studied
them both for a moment, smiling. "Bus was a little late, though,
eh?"

He looked like a sheep farmer. Big hands, broad shoulders,
sandy hair, dark blue coveralls, muscles all over. And a smile
that seemed to cross his whole face. He grabbed both of their
battered suitcases in one hand as if they were toys and started
up the driveway toward the house.

"Kurt and Marianne have been looking forward to your
visit," he called over his shoulder. "We all have. I think you'll
have a great summer with us here."

Peter and Elise had finished classes two weeks earlier, back
in their city of Helsingor. Now they had four more weeks of
vacation to enjoy before school started again in August. Their
parents had put them on the train and told them, "Have fun this

summer. Don't think about the war." Peter was determined to do just that.

As they got closer to the Ringsted farmhouse, Peter could tell it was like many others across Denmark: U-shaped around a gravel courtyard. The bedrooms were usually on one side of the U, the kitchen and living rooms at the top of the U, and an attached barn on the other side of the U. There were a few smaller buildings scattered around that looked like the main building—white stucco walls, thick wooden beams crisscrossing the walls, and a thatched roof. Peter could hear kids' voices coming from the kitchen, through the open window.

"They're here!" a boy yelled. That would be cousin Kurt, younger by one year.

"Of course they're here," came another voice, this one a girl's. That was Marianne, their older cousin by one year. "You don't need to yell."

A heavy wooden door swung open into the courtyard, and a moment later, Peter and Elise were drawn into the middle of the Ringsted country kitchen, surrounded by Kurt, Marianne, Uncle Harald, and Aunt Hanne.

They were immediately bombarded with questions: How was the train ride? How long did it take? Did the ferry rock much? Were there German soldiers all over the country? Were you scared? Did anyone talk to you?

Peter and Elise answered everyone politely, but finally they couldn't keep from yawning. It had been a long day.

"Oh, my." Aunt Hanne put her arms around her niece and nephew. "We've been so excited to see you two that we've completely forgotten what time it is! Are you hungry for dinner?"

Peter and Elise looked at each other. Did fish swim? Their mother had packed them sandwiches and hard-boiled eggs, but those had been finished off hours earlier. Peter could smell sausages and boiled red cabbage cooking on the stove, and it started his stomach rumbling.

"You don't need to answer," their aunt told them. "I know what hungry eleven-year-olds look like. You just sit down, and we'll have dinner."

"Yeah," put in Kurt. "We've been waiting—"

His mother cut him off with a sharp look that told Kurt to mind his manners. Aunt Hanne was as petite as her husband was stocky. She looked small and delicate, even birdlike—but pretty. Kurt took after his father. Though a year younger than Peter and Elise, and two years younger than his sister, he stood slightly taller than any of them. Peter thought he looked out of proportion, though, with a face full of freckles and hair that stuck out in every direction. And when he smiled, his ears wiggled.

"Um, yeah," fumbled Kurt. "We've been waiting for months to see you."

"That's right, Kurt," agreed Uncle Harald, sitting down to eat. "We haven't seen Peter and Elise since they were practically babies, have we?"

Peter nodded and was just about to dig in to the sausage his aunt had put on his plate when Elise kicked him under the table. He looked up, surprised.

Uncle Harald cleared his throat. "Marianne, would you give thanks for us?"

Peter glanced sideways at his sister, but she had her head bowed like everyone else in the room.

"Sure," agreed Marianne. "Dear God, thank you for this good day, and for bringing our cousins here to visit, and for giving them a safe trip. Thank you also for this good food. . . ."

While Marianne was praying, Peter watched his cousins through a crack in his folded hands. Marianne looked so much like Aunt Hanne that Peter almost had to study them to tell the difference. Petite, with dark, braided hair. They even talked alike.

Kurt reminded him a little of his best friend Henrik Melchior,

back home in Helsingor. Only Henrik wasn't there anymore—
not since last October, when Peter and Elise had helped him
escape to Sweden. It had been a long school year since then, and
much quieter without Henrik around.

"Peter?" His aunt was holding a plate of steaming red cabbage in front of him.

"What? Oh, sure, I'll have some more."

Kurt giggled and Peter blushed. Sometimes when Peter
started thinking about something, minutes would go by, and
then he would "wake up." His aunt had probably been holding
that dish in front of his face for a while.

"You must be exhausted from the long trip," Aunt Hanne
said, giving Kurt a stern look. "What time did you leave this
morning?"

"Eight-thirty," Elise answered for him.

"Well, let's get these travelers fed and to bed," said Uncle
Harald. "Kurt and Marianne will show you your beds after dinner, and then tomorrow we can show you around the farm."

————

When Peter saw the cot he was to sleep in, he could hardly
wait to roll under the sheets. It was still light out—and would
be until almost eleven. These were what people called the "Light
Nights," when the sun set late and rose early. But just then, Peter
didn't care if it never got dark. All he wanted was a place to lay
his head.

"I'll be sleeping right over here in the bed," explained Kurt.
"So if you need anything, you can wake me up, okay?"

Peter was too tired to answer. He fell asleep on top of the
covers before he even got his clothes off.

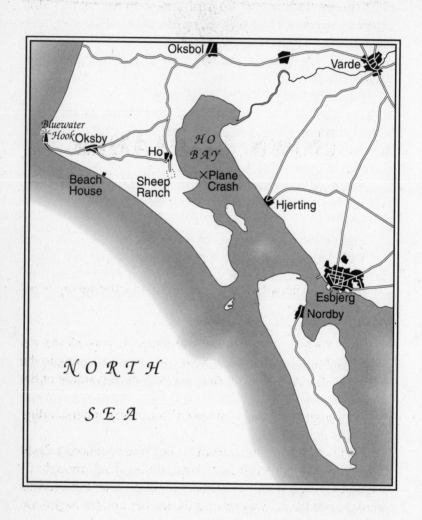

Down in Flames

Peter woke up with a jerk. Someone had fallen on top of his cot in the darkness.

"Sorry," mumbled Kurt.

Peter tried to sit up, to figure out where he was. His cousin rolled off the cot and onto the floor. "I—I was just going to the outhouse. Forgot you were sleeping here in the middle of the floor."

"Let me go with you," answered Peter, finally understanding what was going on.

Kurt fumbled around next to his bed and produced a flashlight. The batteries must have been almost dead, though; he pointed a weak glimmer of light out the door. Peter followed his cousin down the hallway, toward the kitchen and the back door. As they passed Marianne's room, the door cracked open.

"What was all that racket?" whispered Marianne.

"Shh," Kurt whispered back. "I just tripped over Peter's bed, that's all. Go back to sleep."

"No, we have to go, too. Wait for us."

So now the four of them, with Kurt and his near-dead flash-light in the lead, tiptoed out the back door and into the warm night. Since it was completely dark, Peter figured it had to be at least midnight. Maybe later. Once outside, Kurt raised his voice a notch.

"You know where the Big Dipper is, right?" asked Kurt.

"Sure," replied Elise. She pointed up at the sky where the familiar outline of stars pointed north. "And there's the North Star and the Little Dipper, too."

They all stood there for a few minutes, until Marianne started hopping in place.

"It's getting too cold out here, Kurt. Elise and I'll use the outhouse first, then we're going back to bed."

"Oh, come on," replied her brother. "We just got out here."

"It's okay," offered Elise. "A few more minutes is okay."

While the girls carefully made their way along the dark path to the outhouse, Peter studied his new surroundings.

"Which way is the ocean?" asked Peter. "I got my directions mixed up in the bus."

Kurt pointed his light back toward the house. "That way. The water is on three sides of us."

"Like an island?"

"Almost. Bluewater Hook and Oksby are out that direction. That's where our big lighthouse is, too." Then he turned around to face the opposite direction and waved the weak beam toward the outhouse and the woods beyond. "Past those trees is Ho Bay."

"Now I remember." Peter was starting to get the picture in his mind again. They were on a big arm of land, pointing down. The farm was toward the end, where the wrist would be. The bus had taken them through the little village of Ho, and it was kind of a triangle between the farm, Ho, and the Hook.

"Do you think we can go to the beach sometime?" asked Peter.

"Sure!" replied Marianne as she and Elise returned from the outhouse. "We can go down to the bay beach. The ocean beach on the other side is mostly covered with mines and barbed wire, and it looks horrible. Except for a few spots, and we know where those are."

Peter wondered how close they would get to the mines. "Really? I've never seen a mine before."

"Oh, you don't see them," she continued. "And the Nazis don't let you get very close. Since they invaded, they built these big concrete forts into the cliffs, and they're always marching around with their guns and those big mean shepherd dogs. They scare the sheep. Mikkel says they do it on purpose, just to bother us."

"Mikkel?" asked Peter. He had forgotten all about their older cousin, who had not been home for dinner. "Where is he?"

Kurt turned around to face the others and lowered his voice to a hush again. "Can you keep a secret?"

"I guess so," Peter whispered back, wondering why they were whispering. "At least, Elise always can."

"Kurt! Are you sure?" Marianne sounded a little more doubtful, a little more like a mother.

"Sure. They're our cousins, remember?" Kurt lowered his voice even further, as if there were spies in the backyard. Peter had to lean forward to make out what he was saying.

"My brother Mikkel's always out late at night," whispered Kurt. "A lot of times he's out with girls."

Elise giggled. "That's your secret?"

"No! I mean, Mikkel's part of the Underground. If you want to know about any factories or things that are being blown up, Mikkel could tell you. But he doesn't, of course. After chores are done, he's always gone."

Peter thought about his Uncle Morten back home, the only

other person he knew who did that sort of thing. Except now Uncle Morten was probably sitting in a German prison.

"He won't admit anything, though," Marianne added. "And he always tries to be real cool about it. But Mom and Dad know."

"They let him?" asked Elise.

Kurt shrugged. "He's nineteen. What can they do about—"

He was interrupted by a distant, low thunder that sounded like cannons. At first there were a couple of shots, then the night air was peppered by the sounds. There was no mistaking the sound of big guns. Everyone froze.

"Which direction?" whispered Kurt.

Everyone stood as still as statues for a moment. They decided the booms came from the ocean side.

"That way, I think," guessed Peter, pointing toward the house. He had heard guns before but never like this. It sounded as if they were really shooting at something. Then they stopped as quickly as they had started, replaced by a rumbling roar in the distance.

"Now what is it?" asked Marianne, looking up at the dark sky around the farm.

Suddenly they all heard the unmistakable, throaty roar of an airplane, but there were coughs, pops, and explosions, too.

"It's coming from the woods, I think." Marianne pointed. Everyone turned in the direction of the noise. It was getting louder.

They didn't wait long before a flaming comet of an airplane came sputtering and coughing directly overhead. Flames were spurting out of one wing. Even though it was still several hundred feet overhead, they all ducked.

"Whoa!" yelled Peter. "It's going to crash, isn't it?"

He was asking Kurt, but his cousin was already running down the path as fast as he could toward the bay, his flashlight bobbing with him. The three of them stood there, trying to decide whether to follow or run back to the farmhouse.

Kurt stopped at the edge of the woods and shouted back, "Come on! It's going down right over there! In the bay!"

"But we should tell Dad!" Marianne called back. "I'm going back up to get him." She put her hand on Elise's arm. "You two can go back to the house, or whatever. I have to get Dad." Then she disappeared, leaving Peter and Elise standing in the dark yard. It only took them a second to decide what to do.

"Kurt!" yelled Peter. "Wait up!"

Peter could barely see his cousin Kurt, much less the trail. Elise was about ten steps ahead and going around a bend. She looked back just as Peter tripped on a root and fell on his face.

"Hurry, Peter!" she yelled.

Peter didn't need much encouragement; in a second he picked himself up and was right behind her again.

"I can't see a thing," he told her.

"Me neither," agreed Elise. "We just have to keep up with Kurt."

The three of them thrashed through the woods for several hundred yards, and Peter lost track of which direction they were going. The bay was supposed to be close by, he knew, but how close, he wasn't sure. Once in a while, Kurt paused and called back to see if his cousins were following.

Peter leaned over with his hands on his knees, trying to catch his breath. They had been stumbling along for about ten minutes. "Is it much farther?" he puffed.

"It's just ahead," Kurt called back.

A minute later all three were standing out on the mud-flat beach, but there was no plane to see. A small moon cast a pale light on the still water.

"I can't understand it," puffed Kurt. "It couldn't have flown far, the way it sounded."

Peter knew his cousin was right, and he looked a little harder down the beach. Up the bay, to the left, the water ended in more tideflats. Down the bay, to the right, it eventually opened up to the ocean and to Fan Island. As he scanned the shoreline he spotted something in the distance—a flicker of light, a large shape in the water.

"There!" Peter pointed down the bay, and the others followed his direction. "I think I see something."

"Where?" asked Kurt. Peter got a little closer to his cousin, trying to point out where he had seen the light. It flashed again.

"I see it!" said Kurt, and he was off again, trotting along the muddy shoreline.

Peter and Elise scrambled to keep up with Kurt, sometimes sinking in the soft mud, sometimes stepping right into low tide pools. After about fifteen minutes, Peter couldn't tell if they were any closer to where he had seen the light, but he knew they were a lot wetter and a lot muddier.

"Do you see anything?" asked Peter.

Kurt was still leading the way, sometimes walking as fast as he could across the low beach, sometimes jogging. "It's right up here, I'm sure," he called back. "Has to be."

Peter wasn't so sure anymore. They had just arrived at this farm, and already they were on some kind of adventure. What would they do if they actually found a crashed plane? Would they have to rescue anyone?

It was at least ten minutes later when they reached the spot where Kurt thought the lights had come from. They stopped and scanned the water. Nothing. Then Elise pointed to a dark shape almost straight out from them, a little farther than Peter could throw a rock. Another flashlight was bobbing around, its pale light shining on the dark skeleton of a warplane.

The moonlight brightened from behind a cloud, and they could see more clearly. The plane was twisted, nearly upside down, and missing a wing, but it was the same plane they had seen gliding over the farm. It had to be. Whoever had the other flashlight turned around and flashed the strong light back at them.

"Kurt," shouted a man. "Is that you?"

"What?" Kurt shouted back.

"Kurt! You have to find Dad!" the man shouted even louder. "Find Dad, fast! We need some help!"

"Marianne's already getting him."

"Good!" came the answer. By then Peter had figured out that the man wading out to the plane was his oldest cousin, Mikkel, the one who was nineteen. "Then get out of here. Go home!"

"No way!" Kurt stood his ground. "We'll help you."

"No!" yelled Mikkel, but he didn't sound as sure of himself this time.

Kurt turned to Peter and Elise. "That means yes. Come on."

"Sure didn't sound like yes to me." Elise shook her head.

"Believe me," said Kurt as he started wading out after his brother. "It's okay. I know my brother."

Elise grabbed Peter's arm. "You go ahead, Peter, but I'm staying right here on the beach."

Part of Peter wanted to stay on the beach with his sister, which was probably the sensible thing to do, but just then Kurt stumbled in the dark water. Peter jumped out, looking for his cousin. Kurt came up a moment later, struggling in the knee-deep water. It was cold enough to make Peter catch his breath, but he just reached out and grabbed Kurt by the shoulders.

"I'm fine, I'm fine," sputtered Kurt. "Come on."

By now Peter was wet and out in the water, so he continued to follow his cousin. Once he got used to the water, it wasn't so bad, and it got deeper only very slowly. The hardest part was keeping each step from being sucked down in the mud. Both of them pushed through the inky bay as fast as they could make their legs move.

Just ahead, Mikkel's flashlight disappeared into the wreck of the plane. By now the water was over their waists.

The strong smell of gasoline was everywhere, and it worried Peter. Kurt didn't seem to notice as he climbed up on an upside-down engine. Not wanting to stay in the water alone, Peter scrambled up on the plane, too. It had been at least thirty, maybe forty-five minutes since they heard it roar over the farm. Now, even this close, it was hard to tell which end of the plane was up. Kurt pointed his light on the wing, and they could both make out circle markings that looked like archery targets.

"British." Kurt whistled quietly.

Mikkel was clattering around inside, and Kurt pounded on the plane. "We're out here," he yelled.

"You should have stayed on shore," Mikkel yelled back, sounding as if he were inside a huge tin can. Peter could hear Mikkel crawling around inside, and once in a while there was a faint flash of light as he went from one end to the other.

"See anything?" Kurt knocked on the side of the plane again.

"He's gone!" came Mikkel's muffled voice. "The pilot's gone! And so is—"

"And so is who?" asked Peter.

Mikkel said nothing, and it was quiet inside for a moment.

"Mikkel?" asked Kurt. "Are you okay?"

"Yeah, I'm fine," said Mikkel. "Just don't come in here. And listen to me this time."

Kurt slid off his perch next to Peter and sloshed around to the other side of the wreck. At the same time, Mikkel started moving back toward the front of the plane. There was a loud crash from inside, and Peter thought he heard a groan.

"Mikkel?" Kurt yelled. "Mikkel?"

There was no reply, and Peter didn't stop to think what that might mean. In a second, he climbed up on the belly of the plane, lowered himself through an open hatch, and scrambled down inside.

"Mikkel?" Peter felt his way in with his foot. Everything was sideways, giving the plane an eerie angle. The floor was where the side wall should have been, and the side wall was where the floor should have been. He shook his head, trying to figure which way was up. Then he saw Mikkel's flashlight, pointing uselessly off toward the back of the plane. He picked it up and pointed it around. He was staring right in Mikkel's face.

"I thought I told you not to come down here, Kurt." Mikkel shielded his eyes. He was lying underneath a pile of oxygen tanks, each one the size of a large dog.

Peter didn't know what to say and just stood there, shining the big flashlight.

"Well, don't just stand there." Mikkel's voice sounded pained. "Since you're here, you better help me. I got myself squeezed under these tanks pretty good."

Peter moved to pick up a tank. "I'll help you, but I'm not Kurt. He's still outside."

"Hey, Peter." It was Kurt, from somewhere outside the plane. "What's going on in there?"

"We're okay," said Mikkel. "Stay there. I just knocked over some stuff. We'll be right out."

"Are you really okay?" asked Peter. He wasn't sure, the way his older cousin sounded.

"Yeah, I think so." Mikkel shifted his weight and pushed a tank as Peter pulled. "Just a little squeezed in here. And I'm pleased to meet you. The last time I saw you, you were just a baby. Only you should have stayed on shore, the way I said."

Peter didn't say anything but kept rolling the heavy tanks off his cousin. He dragged one to the side, and Mikkel groaned with pain.

"What about the pilot?" asked Peter. "Isn't he here?"

"No pilot. He's gone. Must have slipped out before I got here."

"Nobody else on the plane?" Peter pointed the flashlight toward the rear of the plane.

"No!" Mikkel grabbed the flashlight. "Nobody else."

"Mikkel!" came Kurt's voice, a soft whisper from the open

hatch. "I see lights from trucks coming on the other side of the bay, over by Hjerting!"

"Nazi soldiers, probably," guessed Mikkel. "Get out of here, now! Wade as fast as you can back up to the beach, but keep the plane between you and them, so they can't see you. Dad's probably on the beach by now. I'll follow you."

"Are you sure?" asked Kurt. "Are you okay?"

"I'm fine. Just get back home."

Mikkel took the light as they both pulled away the last tank, and the older boy slipped free. He stretched gingerly, testing his legs. Then he nodded and slapped Peter on the back.

"I'm fine, really," said Mikkel. "Now scoot."

Peter did as he was told, crawling carefully out of the hatch. Kurt was waiting down in the water. On the opposite side of the bay, even though it was about a mile across, Peter could make out headlights and flashlights shining around the beach. He knew who it was, searching for the same thing they had found. *Nazis!*

"Come on," urged Mikkel. "Stay close to the plane and then slip around behind it."

Peter knew they had to get out of the water and back to the other side, fast. But the faster the three of them tried to go through the waist-deep water, the more the mud seemed to pull at their feet. Peter's left shoe came off, but he didn't stop to get it. Halfway back to the beach, he looked over his shoulder.

A searchlight snapped on from one of the German army jeeps on the opposite side of the bay, and Peter froze when he saw its silver beam sweep toward them.

"Mikkel!" he whispered. "A searchlight!"

Mikkel dropped to his knees in the shallow water and dunked Peter and Kurt right next to him. It was barely deep enough to cover them as they lay there, but they didn't move. Peter didn't even think of the bone-chilling cold of the water, only what he would do if he raised his head up and there was a light shining in his face. How long could he hold his breath? His lungs were burning by the time Mikkel let go of him to get a breath. They bobbed carefully back up and looked for the searchlight. It had swept over them and continued on to the plane, where it was now focused. With a sigh of relief, Peter got up and followed Mikkel and Kurt the last few feet to shore.

Just as Mikkel had predicted, Uncle Harald was waiting for them there, out of sight, and he pulled them down as they stumbled behind the bushes. Elise and Marianne were gone.

"I apologize for this terrible way to welcome you to our farm!" said Uncle Harald in a low voice. He put his arm around Peter. "We will have to make it up to you." Then he looked over at his oldest son and spoke almost in a whisper. "The pilot was dead?"

"No, only the crewman," replied Mikkel. Peter understood then why Mikkel had not wanted him to see the back end of the plane. He shuddered at the thought of being in that dark airplane with a. . . . He felt his stomach turn.

"Then where is he?" Uncle Harald sounded worried.

"Quick on his feet, it seems," reported Mikkel, businesslike. "He was gone by the time I arrived, and that was only about half an hour from when he went down. He must have scrambled out pretty quickly and found a place in the woods. But the supply barrels were still in the plane. Only the radio that we needed was gone. That's all they had time to dump, unless the pilot took that with him. But I kind of doubt it. Not enough time."

Peter wondered if he was supposed to hear all that, about the radio, supplies, and the rest. Uncle Harald put his big hand on Peter's shoulder.

"Don't worry about any of this, Peter." Uncle Harald's voice was kind, even as he reprimanded them. "And you, Kurt, you had no business taking Peter out there. It's far too dangerous for you to get involved in this sort of thing."

"I'm sorry, Dad," mumbled Kurt. "We just saw the plane going down, and I thought—"

"No, you didn't think," replied his father. "We'll discuss it later. Right now we need to get you home."

Right then getting back to bed and pulling the covers over his head sounded like a great idea to Peter. His wet clothes clung to his body, he was dripping and shivering, and he only had one shoe. Both feet were covered with mud. He didn't look back to see what was happening at the crashed airplane, only followed between his Uncle Harald and Mikkel on the trail back to the farm through the pine woods. By the light of the flashlight, he noticed Mikkel was limping badly.

"Good thing the tide's coming up," observed Mikkel. "That should cover most of our tracks."

And the pilot's, thought Peter. He couldn't help wondering who the English pilot was, or if he would ever meet him. Probably he was in these same woods somewhere, wishing he were home in bed, too.

Everyone was awake back at the Ringsted farm, and everyone had questions—especially Aunt Hanne. Where was the pilot? Did you see any German soldiers? How did you get all wet?

While Kurt and Peter were drying off, they had to explain every detail. When they got to the part about the searchlight, Aunt Hanne gasped.

"Oh, Peter," she fretted. "Your mother is going to disown me as her only sister when she finds out what you've been through. And here you and your sister were supposed to get away to a nice, quiet holiday at your Aunt Hanne's and Uncle Harald's sheep farm."

Peter tried to grin back at her, but he was afraid she would see how scared he had been. "That's okay. We're kind of used to it."

"Don't tell me you have this kind of excitement every day in the city," asked Uncle Harald, handing them another towel.

"Well, not really," offered Elise. "But last fall—" She looked at her brother.

"You'll have to tell us the whole story," said their uncle, "but right now we have to get you kids into something warm and get you to bed. One-thirty in the morning is not the usual farm bedtime, you know." Then he glanced over at Mikkel, who was washing up at the kitchen sink and looking out the window.

Suddenly Mikkel froze. "Dad!" He threw down his towel. "There's a truck coming up the driveway right now. German, I think."

His father stepped quickly over to the window, pulling back the lace curtain. Then he looked back at Aunt Hanne.

"Hanne, get the kids into their bedrooms. Mikkel, you jump into bed, too. Hurry now!"

Peter and Elise looked at each other, and Peter felt his heart starting to race once more. He hated that feeling. Without a word he quickly followed Kurt into his small bedroom.

Peter stripped off his wet clothes, threw them in a pile under his cot, and dove under the covers. Kurt just took off his muddy shoes and hid under his blanket. They had barely done that when Peter heard a loud knocking at the front door, out by the kitchen.

For the next several minutes, Peter heard German voices— loud voices—as soldiers searched the Ringsted farmhouse. Closets were opened and slammed shut, chairs moved. He could hear voices outside, too, as soldiers went around the building and into the sheep barns. *It's a good thing the pilot's not here*, thought Peter. *Or they would find him for sure.*

The door to their bedroom burst open, and Peter did his best to lie motionless. He could tell, though, when someone shined a flashlight in his face, and he tried to breathe slowly, evenly, as if he were asleep. Slowly, evenly. Deep breaths. The flashlight stayed on his face, and he saw bright red. He didn't move a muscle, but his whole body was tingling. Then he thought about the pile of wet clothes under the bed.

What if they see the wet clothes? That will give it away for sure. Stupid! I should have just kept them under the covers with me!

He heard boots clicking on the bare wood floor as the soldier walked to the other side of the room and opened the closet. Then someone else walked down the hall and stopped at the bedroom door.

"Fritz," came the voice. Peter couldn't understand what the soldier was saying, but it sounded urgent. He did pick out a couple of words, the ones that sounded a little like Danish. "Englander." They were talking about the pilot. The one in the hall said something, then laughed—an unpleasant, throaty sound, almost ugly. There was a shout from the kitchen, and without another word, the two soldiers left.

"Did you hear what they said?" Kurt whispered, when everything was quiet.

Peter let out his breath and opened his eyes, finally. "Yeah, but I didn't get much. You know German?"

"A little. Mikkel knows it better. But I know they were talking about looking for the pilot."

"I figured that," said Peter.

The girls padded in from their bedroom next door. "They're gone," announced Marianne. The dim light from the hall filtered in behind her.

"Yeah," said Kurt. "I was just telling Peter what two of them were talking about in our room while they were poking around."

"What?" asked his sister.

"Well, they were looking for the pilot, and—"

"We know all that, Kurt," said Marianne impatiently.

"Just let me finish. I said they were looking for the pilot, and one of them, the one that was looking in my closet, said something like 'The Englander has got to be here somewhere.' "

"Are you sure?" asked Marianne.

"Yeah," replied Kurt, "I'm sure. Then they said something else I didn't quite understand—something about outside, or looking around outside. And then, listen to this, the one in the hall said he didn't believe that sheep farmer either. 'We'll be back,' I heard him say. 'And we'll catch them at the dinner table having English tea.' "

Peter shuddered at the thought of the soldiers returning. And he wondered again, *What happened to the British pilot?*

3

KURT'S PLAN

When Peter woke the next morning, Kurt's cot was empty, and the sun was shining in through the bedroom window. Trying to wake up, Peter looked around his cousin's room. It was sparse compared to his room at home in Helsingor. There were a few pictures of airplanes on the wall, clipped from magazines, and a large deer antler tied to the headboard of the bed. It made a good hat rack. On the small table next to the bed was a weathered black Bible, one that looked as if it had been tossed around a lot. A knock on the door interrupted him.

"Peter, time to get up," came his aunt's pleasant voice. "It's almost lunchtime."

"Lunchtime?" Peter sat up. "What do you mean?"

"I'm only teasing," she laughed softly from the other side of the door. "I just mean you're the last one in bed. If you sleep in any longer, you might as well stay there until dinner."

Peter liked his aunt already. He looked in his small brown suitcase for some clean clothes, pulled on a pair of blue pants and a wrinkled shirt, and opened the door. Aunt Hanne was just starting down the hall.

Peter looked around and rubbed the sleep from his eyes. "So where is everybody? What time is it?"

She turned to wait for him, and they walked toward the kitchen.

"Out doing chores, just like every day. Your sister got up with Marianne. I think she was surprised you were still sleeping. They were going to wake you up, but I told them to leave you alone. You must have needed it. And it's eight-thirty already."

Peter couldn't remember when he had slept so late. But Aunt Hanne had saved him some breakfast, and he sat down to a bowl of oatmeal, topped with creamy milk and butter. There was bread besides, black rye bread cut in thick slices.

"This is great," said Peter, wolfing down another spoonful of oatmeal. "Even the milk tastes better than at home."

"You like it?" asked his aunt, who was cleaning up dishes in the kitchen sink. "It's goat's milk."

"Whose milk?" Peter gulped. Everything seemed different on this farm. The food, the people, even the way they talked was different. He had to listen carefully to get past his aunt's accent, which was different than the way people spoke back home.

"Goat's milk." She smiled. "You know, little animals with four hooves? We milk a few of them, just for a little extra fresh milk on the table. They run out with the sheep. It's richer than cow's milk, almost like cream."

Peter stopped for a moment, his hand on the pitcher. Then he thought, *Why not?* and poured a little more on his oatmeal.

The big country kitchen was different, too—much different from their kitchen back home in the city. It looked like a farm crew could have a meal at the big, rough table, with room to spare. And everything around him was bright—either white-washed or plain wood. Yellow curtains hung at the window, and the sun streaming in past them made things seem extra bright.

It spotlighted the only dark thing in the room: a black-framed wall hanging with fancy, hand-embroidered lettering. Peter stared at it for a minute, trying to make out the words.

"As for me . . ." he read.

"Joshua," said Peter's aunt.

"Joshua? You mean the Bible Joshua? Or someone in our family?"

She laughed, in a pleasant, warm kind of way that didn't make Peter feel embarrassed.

"I mean Joshua from the Old Testament," she answered. "You know the verse? It's from Joshua, chapter twenty-four: 'Choose for yourselves this day whom you will serve, whether the gods your forefathers served beyond the River, or the gods of the Amorites, in whose land you are living. But as for me and my household, we will serve the Lord.' "

Wow, thought Peter. *She's got it all memorized.* He remembered the Bible on Kurt's table and wondered for a moment if his cousin had it all memorized, too.

"My mother—your grandmother—embroidered that." She pointed out a corner for Peter to see. "See where the last letter isn't quite done?"

Peter looked closer and saw that part of the "d" of "Lord" wasn't quite finished; it almost looked like an "a."

"This was the last thing my mother made before she died," said Aunt Hanne. "Of course, that was years before you were born. She never quite finished this hanging, but I left it the way it was." Then she looked at Peter and smiled. "It reminds me that God isn't finished with me yet, either."

He nodded politely.

"But I'm talking your ear off, Peter. Why don't you run out to the sheep houses and try to find the others? They're probably still cleaning out stalls."

"Okay." Peter pushed out his chair to get up from the table.

"Thanks for the food." No Dane would ever think of leaving a meal without saying that.

"You're welcome," said his aunt. "Now can you find the sheep houses all right? They're off to the side there." She pointed.

Almost on cue, a lamb made a loud bleat just outside the window. "What's that?" Peter jumped out of his chair and went to the window. His aunt just laughed.

"Oh that." She smiled. "I'm surprised it took this long for the little beggar to make it in for breakfast. It's our bummer lamb."

"Bummer?" Peter looked back at his aunt, thinking she was making another joke.

"Bummer lamb," she explained. "Orphan lamb. Its mother died this spring, so we have to give him a little help." She pulled a bottle from the cupboard, carefully filled it with milk, and snapped what looked like a rubber glove over the neck.

"Here." She handed Peter the bottle. "Give it this. He'll drink the whole thing, but he's starting to get used to eating a little more grass. Just don't get too attached to the little guy, like a pet. This is a farm, remember."

Peter took the bottle and headed out the back door. "Sure, I'll feed him."

The little white-faced lamb wasn't shy at all, and seemed to know as soon as Peter's leg was out the door that breakfast was coming. Peter laughed at the cries of the young animal.

"You're ready for breakfast, huh?" He bent over and offered the bottle, and the little lamb hungrily sucked the rubber nipple.

"Hey, not so fast." Peter nearly lost his grip on the bottle. "Go easy." He had never been this close to sheep, and he reached down to pet the coarse wool. The little animal's tail waggled like an airplane propeller as he sucked on the bottle.

After a minute or two, Peter tried to lead the lamb over to where he thought Elise and the others must be, inside the sheep houses. What Aunt Hanne had called the sheep houses were really three whitewashed barns, built to keep sheep at various times. Peter could see the first two were filled with sheep, milling in and out. Quite a few mother sheep—the ewes—had one or two lambs still with them. But the little lamb wasn't interested in going anywhere else; he only seemed to want to stay right there in the courtyard, enjoying his bottle. Finally, Peter wriggled the nipple free and ran toward the nearest barn. The lamb was right at his heels, baaing almost hysterically.

"This way, little guy. Follow me."

Peter didn't have to convince the hungry lamb. It had found its "mother" for the day. When Peter paused for a minute to look around, it caught hold of the nipple again, and Peter let the lamb drink some more. Then a voice came from inside the first barn.

"He has to be here somewhere, Marianne." That was Kurt.

"I know he is," answered his sister. "But who says we have to find him?"

"Yeah, well, if *we* don't, the Germans sure will, right?"

"What does Mikkel say?" asked another voice. *Elise!*

"What does Mikkel say?" said Kurt. "Mikkel never says anything except 'Stay out of this,' or 'Go home.' Just like last night. He thinks we're still five years old or something, and he never lets us know what he's doing. I'll bet he was *waiting* for that plane last night when it crashed. I asked him, but he wouldn't tell me anything. That usually means yes."

By now, the lamb had almost finished the bottle, and Peter managed to slip it out of its mouth again. Then Peter poked his head into the half-opened door of the little barn.

"Anybody here?" he asked.

The three inside were sitting on wooden boxes, between bales of hay, farm tools, and a small tractor. They all looked over at Peter as he walked in, and Kurt waved his hand at him.

"Well, look who's up!" said Kurt. "I thought you were going to sleep all day."

Peter grinned back. It was hard not to like Kurt, even in the short time they had been at the Ringsted farm. He was bossy but always had a smile.

Peter sat down on a crate. "Your mother said you'd be out here doing chores."

"Well, we're out here, anyway," said Kurt. "Almost done with the chores."

Elise looked at her brother, then at the bottle he held behind his back. The lamb was nibbling at Peter's pants, trying to get at the bottle again.

"Who's your friend?" she asked.

The others looked, and Marianne laughed. "Looks like the bummer lamb found a new mama," she said.

Peter looked behind him and lowered the bottle. "Is that all you call him? Just 'the bummer lamb'?"

Kurt shrugged. "Mom and Dad never want us to name the animals. Dad said it'll just make it harder when we have to eat them, or whatever."

Peter remembered what his aunt had said about not getting attached to the animal. It made sense when she said it. Still, the little lamb was so cute. . . . He looked down at the lamb, who was working hard on getting all the milk that remained in the bottle. A little milk splattered out on the animal's nose, and it sneezed. Peter laughed again.

"He sure likes that milk," said Elise, stroking the animal's head. She hadn't ever been that close to sheep before either.

Peter leaned over and whispered in his sister's ear. "How about 'Milky Way'?" he said so no one else could hear. "He likes his bottle so much."

Elise just grinned and nodded. She could keep a secret. Kurt and Marianne didn't notice; they were both studying a drawing Kurt had spread out on his lap.

"Anyway, you're just in time," said Kurt. He made a few notes on his drawing.

Peter leaned over to see. "Just in time for what?"

"Well, we're making a plan." His cousin pointed to his drawing with the pencil stub. "It's a map of where the plane crashed, and where we figure the pilot must be hiding."

Peter patted Milky Way, who had finished his bottle and was just sucking air. "All done, little guy," said Peter. The lamb finally let him pull the bottle away, and Peter studied the sketch. On the left side of the drawing was the ocean and a narrow strip of land. Kurt had penciled in trees and woods, places where there were fields, and the bay on the right side. The land looked just like Peter had pictured it in his head—the giant's arm, with the elbow pointing out to sea, and the hand pointing back toward land. At the elbow and the hand were lighthouses, and toward the bottom of the map was their farm. They were between two small towns, Oksby on the left and Ho on the right, with Ho Bay all the way to the right, and then the land again.

"See, here's where the plane went down." Everyone crowded around as Kurt explained his map. He pointed to a spot just off the beach, in Ho Bay. Peter could still picture what it looked like in the darkness of the night before. Maybe it had been a dream? He wished it had been, but the memory was too clear. Besides, there was still a pile of wet clothes under his bed to prove it. He would have to take care of that when they got back to the house.

"Woods here," Kurt continued, pointing at his map, "and woods here. He has to be somewhere in . . . there." He circled a small patch of woods on the map and marked one spot with an X. "That would be a perfect spot to hide if I were trying to hide."

"Yeah, but you're not," Marianne corrected him. "And don't you think the Germans know all that, too?"

"Maybe." Kurt stood up and started pacing around. "But I don't think so. They don't know the woods like we do. They just go in there with dogs and stuff and crash around. If anyone can find this guy, we can."

Marianne looked as if she wasn't going to let her younger brother get his way. "I still think we should leave it to Mikkel."

Peter and Elise looked up at each other. It looked as if they were going to get involved whether they wanted to or not.

"What do you think, Elise?" Marianne asked her cousin.

Now Elise was on the spot. She looked at Peter again, then at Marianne, then took a breath. "Well, if Kurt knows a few places to look, maybe we should check them out."

"Ha!" Kurt waved the map in Marianne's face and gave her a winning smile. "See?"

Elise's answer surprised Peter, but he didn't say anything. Then he remembered again how she had been the brave one when they were rowing over to Sweden the year before, helping his best friend Henrik escape. She had been the one who kept going, even when he and Henrik had been sick. Peter reached down to pat Milky Way one more time before the little lamb slipped out the barn door.

"All right, then," said Marianne with a sigh. "We'll go out and take a look. But if we run into any German soldiers, I'm coming home right away."

"Don't worry, little sister," said Kurt to his older sister. "We'll stay out of everybody's way. Peter can ride Dad's bike, and Elise can ride Mom's."

On their way out of the barn, though, Uncle Harald stopped them. "Hey, all of you," he called from behind a fence. "I need some help over here! Can you put down your bikes for a few minutes and catch some of these ewes? We're trimming hooves."

The four kids left their bikes on the gravel path and climbed over the pasture gate. Peter stood there with his hands in his pockets, wondering what to do, when Kurt motioned to a group of about twenty sheep huddled in the corner of the pasture.

"Over there," said Kurt, pointing at the flock. "Want to go catch one?"

Peter patted his sister on the back. "We'll give it a try, right, Elise?"

Elise looked at her uncle, who nodded. She and Peter tiptoed across the field, and when the two of them got nearer to the group of sheep, they broke into a careful trot.

But it was no use. The sheep scattered like a flock of birds and were gone to the other end of the small pasture before Peter and Elise even got close.

"Okay," said Peter, scratching his head. "This time you come from the one side, and I'll come around from the other side. We'll both come in at the same time."

"Right," agreed Elise, and she crouched lower as they neared the flock again. They were almost within reach, and Peter crept around to the opposite side.

"Now," signaled Elise, and they zeroed in on the ewe in the front. Peter launched himself in a flying tackle but only came up with a handful of pasture grass.

"Is this how you're supposed to do it?" yelled Peter from the ground. But Uncle Harald, Kurt, and Marianne were only whooping with laughter at the side of the pasture.

"That's great!" Kurt could hardly talk between gasps of laughter. He was clapping his knees and bent over double.

When Peter and Elise realized they were the victims of a joke, they dragged back to where the others were standing. Both tried to keep a grin on their faces.

Peter crossed his arms. "Okay, okay. Pretty good joke. Now you show us."

With a smile and a wink, Uncle Harald dusted his hands off and walked slowly over to the flock. He didn't look at the animals but seemed to be studying the clouds instead. The sheep let him approach this way, and he slowed to a stroll as he came alongside one of the larger ewes. Still looking at the clouds, he crouched down slowly, let his arms dangle, and grabbed the animal's back legs.

"Bring the clippers!" yelled Uncle Harald. In one quick motion, he had the ewe flipped over on her back on his lap, her legs in the air.

The clippers were actually a sharp knife, which Uncle Harald used to whittle off the animal's four overgrown hooves. It was over in less than two minutes.

"Uncle Harald made that look so easy!" exclaimed Elise. "That sheep just lay there like a big wet noodle."

Marianne laughed. "We have to do this pretty often. You'll get the hang of catching them. But whenever someone comes to visit, we have to let them try."

Kurt gave them a salute. "Yeah. Now you've been initiated."

It took them another two hours to finish trimming the sheep, and Peter even caught a few himself. They took turns catching a ewe, then Uncle Harald would trim the four hooves, and they would release the sheep to another pasture. Uncle Harald explained how they had to trim hooves every so often to keep them free from disease. It was a family job.

After the last animal, Peter looked around. "All done," he announced. "That wasn't so hard."

"No, it wasn't," agreed Uncle Harald. "Now we only have two hundred left."

"Two hundred?" Peter couldn't believe it. "Really? Two hundred more . . . today?"

Uncle Harald laughed again. "No, we don't have to do them all today. We can do some more tomorrow. I have some other things to do with Mikkel. You four can go riding now." He waved them on and ambled off toward the house.

Peter sighed with relief, although he hadn't minded the work. It felt good to be helping.

"All right!" Kurt jumped to his feet, ready to go.

"Wait a minute," said Marianne, holding on to Kurt's arm.

Kurt faced his sister, hands on his hips. "What now?"

"It's lunchtime," she replied. "And I'm hungry. Aren't you?"

Kurt frowned, then looked at Peter and Elise. Peter had eaten later than everyone else, but the thought of a sandwich made him feel a bit hungry again, too. *Must have been all that sheep wrestling,* he thought.

"Oh, okay," said Kurt. "But we're never going to get anywhere if we keep fooling around here. Just a quick sandwich."

A "quick" sandwich from Aunt Hanne turned out to be huge slabs of liverwurst on dark rye bread, red cabbage slaw, homemade pickles, and large glasses of cool milk.

"Seems like you've just been here at this table," Aunt Hanne said to Peter.

He smiled up at her and took another bite of his pickle. "Hope you don't mind."

"Mind? Of course I don't mind," she replied. "This is what a farm wife likes to do—feed people. You just have to get used to our jokes."

Elise looked over at her brother, who was finishing the last of his sandwich.

"We already had a good sample of one," she said with a smile.

"Oh?" replied Aunt Hanne. "Uncle Harald didn't send you out to catch sheep, did he?"

Everyone laughed as they cleared the table. Finally, they could leave to ride their bikes. In another minute the four had run outside, picked up the bicycles, and were pedaling down the tree-lined farm road.

"Head for the X!" said Kurt. He waved his map with one hand. Since they were almost at the end of a dead-end road, there was really only one way to go. Soon, Peter remembered, the little dead end would come to the main road, one point of a triangle of roads that went from the Ringsted farm to the little town of Ho and then out to Bluewater Hook and the beaches.

"It's only fifteen minutes from here to Ho," said Marianne.

"Sometimes less if you pedal faster," added Kurt.

Peter didn't say anything as he bumped along at the end of the line, but he had an odd feeling that they were going to find more than they expected.

FOREST SURPRISES

Peter gritted his teeth as he crashed through yet another hole in the gravel road. Marianne looked over at him and grinned.

"How do you like the tires, Peter?" she asked. "Dad made them himself."

"Terrific," he called back. "I have a set back home in Helsingor just like it. Only my tires are made of rope instead of wood."

"Yeah," said Kurt, whose bike had wooden tires as well. "I wish this stupid war would get over soon so we can get some real bicycle tires again. Elise is the only one with a bike that has real tires, and that's just because Mom's haven't worn out yet."

The four of them chattered on like this as they rode along, barely noticing what was going on in the woods around them. Peter shook his head back, squinted up at the sun, and tried not to think about the downed pilot. *Maybe if we just keep riding*, he thought, *all this stuff about soldiers and warplanes will just go away.* He listened to the wind whistling past his face and to Kurt making jokes.

"Did you ever hear of the Molbos?" asked Kurt.

Peter tried to think. This had to be some kind of joke, but he wasn't quite sure. "I don't think so." He turned to Elise. "Have you, Elise?"

Elise just smiled. "Yeah, but I can't remember any Molbo jokes."

Kurt beamed at this chance to tell a story. "How about, did you hear the one where somebody told the Molbos their village was being attacked?"

"Okay, no." Peter waited for the joke. "I haven't heard."

"Well, these Molbo guys wanted to save their bell, their bell from city hall, and—"

"No, Kurt," interrupted Marianne. "If you're going to tell the silly joke, you have to tell it right. The bell was their church bell."

"Church bell, city hall bell, whatever," he said, waving his hand. "So they're trying to save their church bell. And one of them comes up with the idea to take it out in a rowboat and drop it way out in the ocean to hide it until the enemy soldiers leave."

"That's the joke?" asked Elise.

Kurt cleared his throat. "Wait a minute. I'm not done. Anyway, they all think it's a great idea, and so they take the bell down, and row it way out into the ocean, and then they drop it overboard."

"So how did they think they were going to find it, again?" asked Peter.

"That's the joke," Kurt continued. "Because one of the Molbos—you know they're not too bright—said he had the perfect idea. He leaned over the side, took out his knife, and carved a mark in the side of the boat. 'Here,' he says, 'We'll know exactly where we dumped the bell because it's right below this mark.' Everybody thought that was a great idea, and so they rowed home."

Peter laughed, the only one who did. Elise smiled politely,

and Marianne just groaned. Kurt seemed pleased that at least one person liked his joke.

Kurt looked at Peter with a puzzled expression. "You really haven't heard of the Molbos before?" he asked.

"Really," replied Peter. "I guess I'm just not with it."

They were almost to the village, and Peter looked around. The farms were smaller here, and there were more wooded areas, mostly on their left. Peter heard dogs barking, and he looked to see where the sound was coming from.

Through the trees, he saw it clearly: several German soldiers in their drab green uniforms and three huge German shepherds. The dogs seemed to be pulling the soldiers through the trees. It was enough to snap Peter out of his brief minute of forgetting about the war, enough to give him an instant stomachache again.

Then Elise saw it, too. "Look," she said. "What are those soldiers doing in the woods?"

Kurt glanced over and frowned. "What soldiers?"

"In the woods," repeated Peter. "And they have big dogs."

Kurt looked over his shoulder and swerved. "Let's not stop."

Who's he kidding? thought Peter. Stopping was the last thing he had in mind, and he pedaled out ahead as fast as he could. Even with their homemade wooden wheels, Peter and Kurt picked up speed on the flat gravel road, and a minute later they could hear Marianne in the distance, yelling for them to slow down.

"Hey, you guys," she hollered. "Hold up!"

All Peter wanted to do was put as much distance as he could between them and the soldiers with the dogs. He knew the Nazis had to be looking for the pilot. He looked over at Kurt, hoping his cousin wasn't thinking of searching in the same area.

"How much farther?" he asked Kurt as they slowed down to let the girls catch up.

"I think he's closer to the town," his cousin replied. "There's some good places to hide right around Ho, lots of woodsy spots.

Maybe he's even hiding in someone's house."

"You think so?"

"I don't know, but if I were the pilot, I'd find a place to stay pretty quick. Those dogs—" He pointed his thumb behind them where they had passed the soldiers in the woods. "If *they* find him—"

Peter shivered, even though he was hot under the sun. He would never tell Kurt, but he wasn't sure if he really wanted to find this pilot. What would they do with him even if they did find him?

They were passing another thick patch of woods, and Kurt pulled his bike over to the side of the road. He looked behind them, and Peter followed his glance.

"I think we're far enough away," said Kurt. They were at the outskirts of town, and Peter could see several farmhouses clustered together.

"Over there," Kurt pointed toward the town, "is Ho. The pastor lives in that big, long house right there, next to the little church. The one with the big hedge."

Peter and Elise looked at the village. There couldn't have been more than twenty or thirty houses, small, with red-tile roofs and whitewashed outsides. Just like a thousand other farming and fishing villages sprinkled around the little country of Denmark.

"Looks like a nice town," said Peter. "But what kind of a name is 'Ho,' anyway?"

Marianne hopped off her bike. "Who knows? Maybe the first people here grew a lot of hay. You know, ho? Hay?" (The Danish word for "hay" almost sounds like "ho.")

"Or the Vikings used to live here," added Kurt, "and they used to knock you on the ho." He knocked Peter on the head with his knuckles. Not hard, but hard enough to start a little clowning around. Forgetting he had ever seen any soldiers in the woods, Peter dropped his bike in the grass, and they were off, Kurt running for the woods with Peter right behind him.

"I'm going to knock *you* on the ho," yelled Peter, running after his cousin as fast as he could. He glanced over his shoulder to see if Elise would follow. She and Marianne just looked at each other as if they were disgusted with boys. *Maybe they are,* thought Peter, *but who cares?*

Peter was just about to catch his cousin when Kurt ducked behind a tree, and they went around and around, laughing.

"Are you boys just going to play all afternoon, or what?" It was Marianne. Peter was a little winded from running, so he decided it was a good time to give up, anyway. He tried to catch his breath.

"Okay, okay," said Peter between breaths. "Maybe we should get this over with, Kurt. Where did you figure this pilot was again?"

Kurt, looking important, fished his map out of a pants pocket, and unfolded it on a log. Everyone else gathered around.

"We're right about here." Kurt pointed to a place just outside the village. "And there's pretty thick trees all around here." He swept his finger across a section where he had drawn in a small pine tree.

Marianne was having a little trouble deciding which side of the map was up. She turned her head this way and that until finally she caught the right view. "Are you sure he's in here?" she asked. "Why would he be?"

"I told you," said Kurt impatiently. "He has to be somewhere where there are a lot of places to hide, unless he's in someone's house. And I figure he probably headed for lights. You know, like friendly lights."

Peter hoped the man was in someone's house. And he hoped that the Germans with the dogs wouldn't find him. That would be the worst. He tried to push away the knot in his stomach again and listen to his cousin.

"Maybe we should split up and walk toward the village," suggested Elise.

Kurt turned his thumb in the air. "Great! We can meet in the pastor's garden." He pointed ahead, toward the parsonage at the edge of the woods. "Up that way, in about ten minutes."

But Marianne just stood where she was, putting her hands on her hips. "I'm not going to go thrashing through the woods by myself, Kurt Ringsted, not without—"

"Oh, I didn't mean alone," interrupted Elise. "We should go two by two."

Peter was glad Marianne had mentioned it first. Kurt looked around again.

"Right," said Kurt. Then he looked over at Peter. "Come on, Peter."

Peter thought about the soldiers with the guard dogs, somewhere in the woods in back of them. They were a little ways off, and he didn't know which direction the soldiers were going, but he wondered what he would do if he heard the dogs. Run for the pastor's house? Get back on his bike?

"Look, here's a good place to hide," whispered Kurt, holding on to Peter's arm. There was a little hollow between two trees. Two more pine trees had fallen, and there was a low spot underneath. *Maybe a place where an animal would hide*, thought Peter. *Or a pilot.*

The boys tiptoed up cautiously, trying not to make a lot of noise. It didn't look like anyone had been there lately, but maybe. . . . Peter peeked underneath, not daring to put his nose down too far into the hole, where he couldn't see. He could feel goosebumps on his neck. Kurt, for all his talk, wasn't looking any braver but kept close to Peter.

From behind, Peter heard twigs break. He didn't wait to find out who it was but yelped and dove over the log. Kurt was right there next to him.

When he didn't hear anything else, Peter was the first to peek up over the log. He half expected a German soldier, but instead he saw a man standing there in front of the log, staring straight at him. He had dark, unkempt hair sticking up at all angles, and one of the largest noses Peter had ever seen. He was not at all good-looking, but had the pleasant expression of an absent-minded professor.

All Peter could do was force a half-smile, feeling foolish. "We heard something behind us," he started to say, "and we thought—"

By then Kurt had popped up, and he recognized the man immediately.

"Pastor Kai!" said Kurt. "Boy, am I glad it was you. We thought it was someone else—"

The man broke out into a big, hearty laugh. "Sorry to startle you boys," he said. "I was just out for a walk, and I heard noises, so I came to see what it was. Apparently it was you, Kurt, playing hide-and-seek."

"Well, no, not exactly." Kurt stood up and brushed off his clothes. "We were out looking for something."

"Oh?" The pastor seemed interested. "Maybe if you tell me what you lost, I can help you find it. But you have to introduce me to your cousin first."

Kurt stammered for a minute, and Peter guessed his cousin was trying to decide if he should tell the whole story. But how did the pastor know who he was?

"Oh, yeah, sorry." Kurt waved his hand at Peter. "This is my cousin Peter, from Helsingor. His twin sister, Elise, is here somewhere. We were supposed to meet at your house in a few minutes, if we didn't find—" He looked around again. "If we didn't find the British pilot who crashed in the bay last night."

The pastor arched his eyebrows as if he hadn't heard about the pilot. But with all the commotion the night before, the big guns and the sound of the airplane, Peter thought everyone in the town must have known.

"Pilot?" The pastor looked puzzled. "You really do need a hand, don't you? Tell me about it, and we'll head back to the parsonage for a snack. Mrs. Steffensen just baked some bread, I think."

Kurt and Peter told Pastor Kai a short version of their story as they walked toward the parsonage. Elise and Marianne were waiting on the pastor's well-kept lawn, and they looked surprised when they saw the pastor with the boys.

"Look who I found hiding in the woods!" called the pastor.

The boys looked sheepish, as if they had been caught stealing candy from a store. Then Pastor Kai looked at Elise with a friendly smile. "And you must be Elise Andersen." He gave a slight bow. "I've heard good things about you from your Aunt Hanne. Why don't you all come into the kitchen?"

Elise just blushed, but she followed everyone else into the large house.

"You're quite the student, she says," continued the pastor.

"Gifted," put in Peter. "Back home, we call her the Brain."

"Peter!" Elise gave him a sharp look. "You hush!"

Peter and Elise went through another round of introductions with the pastor's wife, who had brought out a plate full of home-baked bread and jam. Just like he had forgotten breakfast when it was time for lunch, now Peter completely forgot the lunch they had eaten back at the Ringsted farm. He decided that people out in the country certainly ate better than he was used to.

The pastor's wife was pretty—like his own mother, Peter thought—only with short-cropped brown hair and what appeared to be a built-in smile. Of course, it was the jam that caught his attention.

"Wow, strawberry jam!" said Peter. "We haven't had jam like that since before the war, when we were little kids."

Mrs. Steffensen set the plate on the kitchen table and stood back. "Homemade," she said. "It's not real sweet, but that's because we couldn't get any sugar this month."

All four of the kids thought it was perfect, and Peter enjoyed three thick pieces of the homemade bread with as much jam as each piece could hold. There were small plums from the yard, too. Mrs. Steffensen smiled as she watched them eat. The pastor ate his piece of bread, then got up from the table.

"Hey," he asked, wiping the jam from the corner of his mouth with a napkin. "Does anyone here like to write poetry?"

"She's the best in the school." Peter pointed at his sister. Elise was in the middle of a bite, so she couldn't argue. She only waved her hand at him, trying to get him to stop.

"Great," replied Pastor Kai as he walked down the hall to his study. "Then I have something for you."

He returned a minute later with a tablet in his hand.

"I'm trying to complete this poem, but I'm stuck on a line. That's why I was out walking in the woods—to clear my mind. Maybe you could help me with a good ending. It's supposed to be part of a sermon I'm working on."

Elise blushed, but took the tablet the pastor gave her, and read a few lines to herself.

"Out loud, Elise," said Peter. "Read it out loud."

She looked around again, cleared her throat, and began.

"I waited patiently through the spring, knowing it couldn't live long. When a frozen blue flower, this delicate thing . . ."

She read some more quietly, paused a minute, smiled a couple of times to herself as she came upon lines that she liked. Then she looked up.

"I like it," said Elise. "It's about garden flowers, but something else, too. Right?"

"You're a poet, all right." The pastor smiled. "And that's where I'm stuck. I need another line about hope. What rhymes with 'spring'?"

"Wing . . . bring?" suggested Kurt.

"How about string?" asked Marianne.

"Okay," said Elise. "But it has to have something to do with hope."

"Hope?" asked Peter. He wasn't so sure about all the deeper meanings. "I thought it was about gardening."

"Well." The pastor took back his notebook. "Same thing, really. I planted the flowers there last fall, hoping for the time when they would come up and bring a little color with them. If you like poetry, you can think of all kinds of things that are like planting flowers. All kinds of things we hope for. You know— spring, or peace, or for the Nazis to take their guns and go back home to Germany."

When the pastor explained it that way, it made a little more sense to Peter.

"Kai," scolded his wife. "You don't have to be telling these kids here about war things. They've probably heard enough already."

"It's okay." Elise smiled at Mrs. Steffensen. Then she turned to Peter. "We'll have to think of something, right, Peter?"

"Sure." He finished off another piece of bread with jam. "Flowers. Rhymes with 'hope.'"

"No," she corrected him. "Hope, but it has to rhyme with 'spring.'"

"Whatever."

All this time, Kurt was looking out one of the kitchen windows, seeming a little anxious. Finally, he cleared his throat. "We really have to go." He looked around the room, as if there might be spies in the hallway. "Have to find that pilot."

The pastor scratched his chin, thinking. "Yes, the pilot," he mumbled.

His wife looked at him, puzzled. "What pilot are we talking about?" she asked.

Pastor Kai looked over at Kurt, as if looking for permission to tell a secret. Kurt nodded.

"I'm sorry, Ruth," said the pastor. "Here we are talking about poetry, and we haven't told you about why the kids are really here. It appears a British plane crashed in the bay last night, and the pilot is still missing."

"Missing?" asked Mrs. Steffensen.

"Yeah," put in Kurt, a little more excited, "and I . . . we think we know where he might be hiding."

The pastor's wife clapped her hands together. "So that's what all the soldiers have been doing this morning! There have been so many trucks going back and forth." Then her expression turned serious, and she looked at Marianne and Elise, who were still sitting at the kitchen table. "You girls should keep track of Kurt, though. I'm not sure it's such a good idea to be roaming around in the woods with all those soldiers."

Marianne smiled. "We're keeping him out of trouble, I think."

There was a noise out in the hallway—a small cough—and everyone turned to see the Steffensens' little seven-year-old boy, trying to hide.

"Jakob," said his mother, "what are you doing out there? Spying on us? I thought you were next door, playing with Olga."

Little Jakob, dark-haired and blue-eyed, came shyly out of his hiding place. He looked guilty.

"I was playing with Olga, Mom, but she had to leave."

"So you've been standing out there, just listening?" asked Pastor Kai. "You should have come in."

"I'm sorry." The little boy looked at his feet for a moment, then peeked up curiously at Peter and Elise. "I just wanted to hear about the English airplane."

The pastor shook his head, with a half-smile that said, "What can you do about seven-year-olds?" Peter smiled, too, as the pastor introduced his son. But Kurt was still anxious, wanting to get out the door.

"We have to go," announced Kurt.

"Thanks so much for the jam and bread," Marianne and Elise

said together, not forgetting their manners.

"Yeah," echoed Peter. "Thanks."

But little Jakob wasn't going to let them go that easily. "If you want to find the pilot," he said as they moved for the door, "why don't you just pray?"

Peter stood still for a moment, embarrassed. *Maybe nobody heard that*, he thought.

When no one said anything right away, Jakob went to his father and started tugging on his hand. "Why don't you?" came the insistent little voice.

"Jakob." The pastor bent down to child level. "The kids are just leaving. I'm sure they'll pray." He held his little son's hand as Elise, Marianne, Kurt, and Peter filed toward the door.

"No, I mean right now," insisted the little boy. "All we have to do is pray, and God will answer, right?"

"Well, son." The pastor fumbled for words. "It's not always that easy. Let's let the kids leave, and we can talk about it some more."

"But they're not going to find any pilot unless they pray!" By now the seven-year-old was on the verge of tears, and everyone looked down at him, not knowing what to do. Peter didn't know what to think of this unusual little boy. But in a small way, it reminded him of his Uncle Morten back home, the one who talked to him about praying, the one who insisted on praying in a room full of Jews their family had been hiding. *But what's he going to think if nothing happens after he prays?*

Pastor Kai crouched down and looked straight in his son's face. "Listen, Jakob, it's not so simple. God may have other plans, or He may choose to answer in other ways. It's just not—"

"But you've always said we should pray about everything," said Jakob. He was not going to let go of his idea.

The pastor looked up at everyone, sighed, and looked back at his son. Then he smiled. "You're right, Jakob. We should pray. Right now? You go ahead, then."

"Okay." Jakob switched right back to a happy face, the way only a seven-year-old can. He folded his hands in front of him, bowed his head, and closed his eyes. "Dear Father, please help Kurt, Marianne, and . . . and . . ."

"Their cousins," his father whispered.

"And their cousins find this Englander who fell down in his airplane. Not the mean soldiers in the ugly uniforms. Amen."

And that was it. Pastor Kai straightened up from where he was crouching next to his small son, and Jakob looked at everyone cheerfully.

"Okay," announced the little boy as if everything were already settled. "You can go find him now."

Peter smiled, still remembering his Uncle Morten. *Wouldn't it be nice if it were so simple?* he thought.

"We'll see you all in church tomorrow?" The pastor turned to Peter and Elise, who looked at each other uncertainly.

"Sure," Marianne answered for them. "And they'll be around for the rest of the summer, too."

"Great." Pastor Kai opened the large front door. "Then we'll have a chance to work on that poem."

Elise smiled. "That will be nice."

The pastor put his bony hand on Kurt's shoulder as they walked out to the front step. "Just one thing, Kurt. You must promise me that you will stay clear of any German soldiers. If you see any, you just go the opposite direction, fast."

"We promise," said Peter, without thinking.

Kurt just looked over at him, then back at the pastor. "Okay, we promise," he echoed.

Peter was just stepping down to the front walk when Jakob squealed. "Look!" he said, pointing excitedly to some distant trees. "What's that up in those trees?"

Everyone followed his pointing to a thicket of pines, past the clearing on the edge of the parsonage property. When Peter saw it, he caught his breath. A parachute, caught in the branches!

They all ran over to the tree, even the pastor. When they got there, they could see the olive-drab parachute had snagged on the upper limbs of the tree, and a small cannister was hanging on a lower branch. They had walked right past that tree before and hadn't seen the parachute!

"What is it?" asked Marianne, staring up at the tangled web of parachute, small ropes, and the cannister.

"Probably a supply drop, maybe from the same plane that crashed," guessed Pastor Kai. "Don't you think, Kurt?"

Kurt shaded his eyes as he looked up at the branches. "My brother said they were looking for a radio. This has to be it."

"Well, there's only one way to find out," said Peter, hoisting himself onto the lowest branches. In a minute, he was up in the tree, pulling at the parachute, untangling it from the highest branches. About the size of a small garbage can, the cannister turned out to be lighter than he thought it would be.

"Maybe it's empty," Peter called down, hanging onto a branch with one hand.

"Peter, be careful," said Elise.

After a few more minutes of untangling, Peter finally freed the parachute, and lowered the cannister down to the ground by the ropes.

Pastor Kai looked around nervously, but there was no one in sight around the parsonage grounds. "Come on," he said. "We can't open this thing up out here. You never know when uninvited guests might arrive." Peter thought of the soldiers, too.

With the pastor in the lead clutching the cannister, Marianne and Kurt followed, holding the crumpled parachute and all the ropes.

"Mrs. Steffensen isn't going to like this," the pastor went on. "But we'll find a place for it in the basement, at least until someone else claims this thing."

"This thing" turned out to be a radio, packed carefully inside the cannister with straw. There was a set of earphones, batteries, even a Morse code blinker switch. Everyone oohed and aahed when the pastor spread it all out on the kitchen table.

"Kai." Mrs. Steffensen crossed her arms. "There is no way we're going to keep all these things here in the house, you know."

The pastor looked over at Marianne and Kurt. "Your brother Mikkel would know exactly what to do with this radio."

They nodded. Peter noticed that the pastor didn't come right out and say that Mikkel was involved with the Underground, but he seemed to know it.

"Then we'll hide this other stuff in the basement, Ruth," said the pastor, gathering up the parachute and ropes and handing them to his wife. "Maybe you can even make a new dress with it." He smiled but his wife only returned a frown. "And this radio here; I imagine someone will be very glad to receive it as soon as possible."

Then he looked down at his son, who was studying the radio. "Well, Jakob, we didn't find the Englander yet, but we found his radio, didn't we?"

The little boy looked over at Peter with total confidence. "See?" he said. "I prayed. God can do anything. We'll find the Englander, too."

Peter smiled back and shook his head. *Maybe the little boy was right*, he thought. After what he had seen in the last twenty-four hours, it didn't seem so impossible.

ROADBLOCK

"You didn't see any German patrols on the way over, did you?" asked Pastor Kai. They were out in the parsonage carriage house, and the pastor was wrapping the radio back up in a carton. On top, he placed blankets and some clothes, then carefully tied the package together with heavy twine. It was a little large for carrying on the back of a bicycle, but it balanced on the pastor's back wheel rack just fine.

Marianne answered for the group. "There were some out in the woods with dogs."

"But no one on the road," added Kurt.

"Good," replied the pastor. "I don't think we want to meet any, just this time." He gave his package another turn of twine and pulled it tight. "There. That's going to stay until we can get it to your brother."

Over his wife's objections, Pastor Kai had insisted that they take the radio immediately to Mikkel. The ride was an easy one, he said, and no one would question a pastor riding with a package for one of his parishioners, especially in the middle of the day, and especially not with a convoy of four young people.

"Come on, kids," said the pastor. "Are you ready for this delivery?"

Peter liked the pastor for his easygoing ways. Still, it worried him a little. He wasn't used to a pastor who was so . . . well . . . *involved*.

Kurt took the lead on the road out of town, followed by Pastor Kai, then Peter, Elise, and Marianne. The girls chatted nervously and smiled, but Peter felt even more tense. *What will happen if we're stopped?* he worried. Even though there had been no soldiers on the road on the way over, it could happen just like that. The soldiers back home in Helsingor would just stop everyone who came along on a road, ask for identification, check papers, sometimes search people. They were usually rude, he thought. He hated the roadblocks, the feeling that something terrible could happen at any time.

"Hey, Peter," said Kurt. "Race you to the next bend in the road!"

The next bend was in the middle of a small patch of woods, several hundred yards away. Kurt was a strong pedaler, but Peter could still keep up pretty well.

"Okay, Kurt," Peter said, picking up the challenge. "On three. One, two—"

"THREE!" Kurt joined in, and the two were off, pedaling as fast as their wooden tires would let them. The gravel road was especially bumpy here, and the ride was rough, but Peter started to pull ahead. He was several bike lengths ahead and almost to the bend in the road when he glanced back over his shoulder. Kurt skidded out of control on a patch of gravel but caught himself. Still, he had to stop.

"You win!" yelled Kurt. By then Peter had made it to the woods. He looked up ahead, around the bend in the road, and caught his breath. By the side of the road, he saw a camouflage-painted German army car. Two soldiers were leaning against it, smoking. They both looked up at Peter, and for a second he froze in fright.

He wished he could turn around, race back, and tell Pastor Kai, who could make a quick U-turn and go home. But that was silly, he thought. They had seen these kinds of army cars a hundred times before. Still, he felt his hands suddenly get clammy on the handlebars. Trying not to act unusual, he stopped his bike and pretended to adjust the chain. *Where is everybody?* he thought. *They ought to be catching up by now.*

Peter heard his sister's laugh as the group got closer. Kurt was telling another of his terrible jokes.

"And then," said Kurt, his voice booming, "here's the funny part. When the Molbos got back to their city—" He stopped in the middle of his punch line when he saw the soldiers. Everyone else saw them at about the same time. Peter didn't wait for anyone to say anything, he just started up on his bike again, and tried not to look up. It was too late to do anything else.

"Just ignore them," whispered Pastor Kai. "Keep riding and ignore them. Don't say a word."

Which is what they all did. Everyone tried to pretend the soldiers weren't there, but Peter felt his grip on the handlebars tighten.

"So what did the Molbos do when they got back to the city?" asked Marianne.

She's brave, thought Peter.

They were almost up to the car, and the soldiers were still standing there. Kurt didn't answer her.

"Guten Tag," said the younger of the soldiers, in a voice loud enough for everyone to hear. Then he repeated himself in Danish: "Good day."

No one said anything, just looked straight ahead. Without moving his head, Peter looked over at his sister. She had her lips pressed tightly together, and she looked as nervous as he felt. A minute later they were around the bend from the two young soldiers, and everyone caught their breath.

"I don't like that," said Marianne. "Why do they always try to pretend they're being friendly?"

"That's just part of their program here in Denmark," replied Pastor Kai. "We're supposed to be grateful to them for coming in and taking over the country. 'Isn't that what neighbors do?' they ask. And then they can't figure out why they get the cold shoulder."

The words were just out of his mouth when Peter, now at the front of the line again, saw something even worse than before. This time it was two trucks and a German army motorcycle. Their worst fear. A roadblock to check travelers.

Peter looked back over his shoulder, but he didn't need to say anything. He could hear the pastor's quiet groan. To make things worse, the jeep from behind them came roaring up the gravel road just then. One of the soldiers stood up as the vehicle slowed to a stop behind the bikes. It was the one who had tried to say hello to them.

"Aufmachen!" barked the soldier, with a sweeping motion of his hand. Peter knew what that word meant: "Get going!" The camouflage-painted car idled as everyone looked at one another. This time the pastor smiled at the Germans and waved his hand back.

"I believe he expects us to continue our ride," he said to the others out of the corner of his mouth. "We seem to have no choice but to get going."

Trying to look as casual and unafraid as they could, Marianne and Kurt pedaled a little faster. The pastor, with his dangerous package on the back of his bike, did the same. Peter and Marianne stayed beside him, while the army car idled along behind.

"Aufmachen," phooey! thought Peter, feeling annoyed at the soldiers. If they had just passed them a little earlier, the pastor

would have been able to turn around. Now they were trapped, and the roadblock was right in front of them. The pastor glanced sideways at Peter and Marianne as they approached the road-block. He really did look as if he were just out on a casual ride with four young friends.

"Don't forget," said the pastor, in a voice that Peter could barely hear over the sound of the car behind them. "You're not aware of my package. Do you understand?"

Peter nodded. He could feel his hands getting clammy again.

Elise only said one word to Peter as he glanced over at her. She said it silently, but he made out the word clearly: "Pray!"

Peter looked back at the road. Was it only an hour before when the pastor's little boy had insisted that they pray for the British pilot? Jakob had been so sure of himself, the same way his Uncle Morten back home had always been.

Up ahead, a young, sharp-featured German officer in a gray uniform held up his hand, motioning them to stop. The brakes on the jeep in back of them squealed as it slowed down.

"Ausweis, bitte," said the officer, motioning with his hand. "Papieren." He was asking to see the pastor's identification card. The kids, under age sixteen, still weren't required to carry one, so they sat there on their bikes, waiting and fidgeting.

The pastor pulled his small card from his wallet and handed it over to the German. This wasn't the first time Peter had been through one of these checkpoints, but he had never felt quite so nervous. *What if?*

Without bowing his head or closing his eyes, Peter knew what he had to do.

God, you just have to protect Pastor Kai, please, he prayed. *Please help us get through this roadblock without the Germans finding out about the radio.*

The officer looked at the small picture on the card, then up at the pastor's face, and back down at the card. Finally satisfied, he handed it back. Then he glanced curiously at the large package tied on the back of Pastor Kai's bicycle.

"Was ist das?" he asked in German, poking at the package. "What's this?"

Pastor Kai acted as if it were just a package of laundry instead of a British radio transmitter that would send him to prison, or worse.

"Oh, that," said the pastor, waving his hand casually. "There are clothes in there. A gift for a needy church member." And it was true, there were clothes in the package, too. He tried to explain to the officer by repeating the Danish word for clothes, pulling at his own shirt, and then pointing at the package. But the Nazi wasn't satisfied.

"Open it," ordered the soldier. Peter was afraid to look. As the pastor pulled at the string, Peter prayed even harder than he had before. *Please, God. Do something!*

Pastor Kai had barely begun to pull open the lid of his package when another army car came up to the roadblock, this one a large black sedan with red swastika flags waving from the front fenders. An officer! The German inspecting Pastor Kai's package snapped to attention, barely casting a glance at the pastor as he gingerly pulled out a shirt. Then the inspector looked over at the scared group of Danes. He paused for a moment, looked at the car, and waved his hand, shooing them away.

"Aufmachen! Go!" he ordered them. For once, Peter was glad to obey. Pastor Kai hurriedly stuffed the shirt back into his package, wrapped the twine around the box again, and jumped back on his bike.

"The man said go," whispered the pastor. "So let's go."

They went, and even Marianne pedaled a little faster. No one said a word until they were well out of sight of the roadblock, and the big black car had long since passed by.

"What would you have done if they had seen what was really inside the package?" Peter asked Pastor Kai.

"To tell you the truth," said the pastor, "I'm not sure. But I was praying, weren't you?"

Peter nodded. "Yeah, I was." It was a different feeling but a good one.

"I know this sounds odd," said Elise, who had pedaled up a little closer. "But all the time we were praying there at the road-block, I had a sure feeling that they weren't going to find the radio. I just knew it."

Strange, thought Peter as they pulled into the long driveway leading up to the Ringsted farm, *but I think maybe I had the same feeling, too.*

The Ringsted kitchen seemed like Christmas in July when Pastor Kai started to unwrap his package on the large table.

"Tell us again how you found it," said Uncle Harald, who had come in from the fields to see what was going on.

"Dad, you should have seen it," explained Marianne. "Little Jakob was spying on us when we were talking in the pastor's kitchen, and then he came in and wanted to pray."

"Yeah," put in Kurt, "and at first nobody really wanted to and everybody was kind of . . . because we just thought . . . you know, 'Oh, come on, Jakob.' But then Pastor Kai told him okay, that we should go ahead and pray."

"Whoa, slow down!" Uncle Harald laughed. "I think I caught what you just said, Kurt." Then he looked straight at Peter. "And that's what you did?"

"That's what we did," Kurt went on. "Little Jakob prayed his own prayer just like he knew what he was talking about. Then we opened up our eyes and walked outside, and there it was—just like that. Peter climbed up in the tree, and we got it down, and here it is."

Marianne looked at her brother. "But we didn't just bring it here, don't forget."

Roadblock 63

Peter hoped they wouldn't get into that again, the part about the German roadblock. But that's when Pastor Kai spoke up.

"No, we didn't just bring it here," interjected the pastor. "And that's where I have to apologize. I thought I could bring this radio over here for Mikkel without any question. I haven't seen roadblocks around here before, at least not like the one we ran into."

"Roadblocks?" Aunt Hanne raised her eyebrows. "There was a roadblock?"

"Yes," continued the pastor. "And I'm sure it must have had something to do with the missing pilot." Then he half smiled. "But the children here were praying, and we seemed to get through just fine. Right, Peter?"

Why does everybody keep asking me about praying? thought Peter. He looked at the floor, then up again.

"We were praying," explained Peter, and it seemed as though it was someone else speaking. "We were praying. I think it, uh . . ."

There was a pause, then Aunt Hanne looked at Peter.

"You think?" she asked, looking for the rest of his thought.

"I think it made a difference," Peter finished, then turned toward the door. He didn't get out, though, as Mikkel pushed through from outside. The older boy was dirty and sweaty, and looked as though he had been crawling through a ditch or something. He was scowling, worse than usual.

Peter tried to get out of the older boy's way, but he moved the wrong direction, and they bumped.

"Sorry," Peter apologized.

Mikkel just grunted and tried again to get through the kitchen door.

"Find anything?" asked Kurt, noticing his brother.

"Nothing. Not a thing. Zero." He spit out the words, to no one in particular. "I don't know where that dumb pilot is, or why he's hiding. The only thing we know is that there are too many Nazis out there, beating the bushes."

Pastor Kai spoke up from the other side of the table. "Yes, as a matter of fact, we ran into a couple ourselves."

Mikkel looked past Peter and noticed the pastor for the first time. "Oh, Pastor Kai, I didn't realize you were here." When he saw his father, in from the fields, and the small radio unpacked on the table, his eyes grew wide. "What's this?"

"Look what we found, big brother," said Kurt, holding up the transmitter. "Pretty good, huh?"

"Careful with that," said Mikkel. He stepped over to the table and took the radio from Kurt, but he was obviously pleased. He turned it around in his hands, looking at it from all sides. "I can't believe you found this. We thought for sure it was gone, or the Germans had picked it up. When it wasn't in the plane, all we knew was that they had dropped it out before the crash."

"Well," said Uncle Harald. "There it is. Now I suggest you take it so that your mother can use her kitchen table again."

Mikkel didn't waste any time gathering up the equipment in the carton. He disappeared out the back door, leaving everyone standing. Aunt Hanne pulled out her large soup pot and started gathering ingredients for a stew. She had piles of carrots, cabbage, beans, and early potatoes from the garden.

"Can you stay for dinner, pastor?" she asked. "It won't be for another few hours, but you're most welcome."

Pastor Kai looked down at his watch and hesitated. "I'm tempted, but I'm afraid I'll have to pass for today. My wife is expecting me home, and she'll worry. And I confess, I still have a few lines left on tomorrow's sermon that need polishing."

"Of course." Aunt Hanne returned to her slicing.

"Perhaps tomorrow after church, then?" asked Uncle Harald. He was heading back out the door to finish his work before dinner. "Hanne's stew is always better the second day, and you can bring your whole family along."

Pastor Kai smiled. "That's okay with the cook?" He looked over again at Aunt Hanne.

"Of course, Pastor." She smiled and nodded.

"Well, then, how can I say no? We'll stop by after church."

Peter watched the men parade out the front door, and Uncle Harald turned as he left. "I'll be back in before six-thirty," he told Aunt Hanne.

"Dinnertime?" Elise asked her aunt.

"No," replied Aunt Hanne. "That's what time the BBC comes on, if we can catch it." She smiled at her niece. "Your uncle wouldn't miss it for anything."

Neither would Mikkel. After another couple of hours working on fence posts with his father and the four kids, he stomped in at six twenty-five, wiping the mud off his hands. He was the last one in; everyone else had come in a few minutes earlier after washing up at the pump in the courtyard. Aunt Hanne gave her oldest son a stern look.

"You may be nineteen years old, Mikkel," she said, "but you still have to clean up, just like everyone else."

"Mother!" said Mikkel. "It's just about to start!"

Kurt motioned for Peter and Elise to sit in the living room, and Uncle Harald took his seat by the large mahogany radio in the corner. It was as large as an adult's backpack, curved at the top, trimmed with fancy carved wood. A lot like their radio at home, Peter thought.

"Your mother's right, Mikkel," agreed Uncle Harald, looking over his shoulder. "You should at least run out and scrub off the worst of it." He fiddled with the dial as Mikkel sprinted outside. Peter felt as if he were waiting for the curtain to rise in a theater instead of waiting for the radio news in a small farmhouse. Everyone sat on the edges of their chairs, waiting for the familiar introduction to the British station, the one that would tell them the truth about what was happening in the war, and in the rest of the world.

Instead, all they heard was the droning sound of an engine, the loud and annoying sound that told them the Nazis were interfering with the radio signal.

"Aww, they're jamming it again," moaned Kurt. Mikkel burst in from outside, shaking his wet hands off.

"Is it coming in?" he asked. Everyone just looked at him, and he heard the grinding, wavering engine sound. "Guess not."

"Quiet!" Uncle Harald shushed them from his perch by the radio. "Let me see if it's over here." He fiddled with the dial, and everyone kept still.

Marianne leaned over to Elise and pointed up at the map of Europe Uncle Harald had pinned on the wall by the radio. "Whenever he hears anything about the war," she whispered, "he puts these little pins in the map where something is happening. We have to sit quiet for a whole hour. It's boring."

Her father put his finger to his lips. "Shh! Here it is."

He was right. Peter heard the familiar opening notes of Beethoven's Fifth Symphony, the ones that announced the BBC news. Aunt Hanne clapped her hands in anticipation.

"Here is the BBC from London," said the announcer in Danish, "sending to Denmark."

Although his family back home in Helsingor wasn't as loyal in listening to the programs, Peter's own father would often tune in the broadcast. Uncle Harald, though, looked as intense as a soccer fan at the European championships. Peter could tell this was serious.

"Tonight," said the announcer, "we bring you a special broadcast from the Prime Minister of Great Britain, Mr. Winston Churchill . . ."

"Churchill himself!" Uncle Harald clapped his hands, obviously delighted to hear the English leader. Then everything was quiet in the room, except for the tinny radio voice of the Prime Minister. Peter and Elise tried to follow along as he spoke about Hitler, the Russians, the French, about the battles they were fighting, and about what a terrible war it was. But it was a little harder to understand this time, since Churchill was speaking in English. So they sat politely, trying to look interested. Peter's mind wandered to the woods, and he thought of the British pilot. *That pilot*, thought Peter, *should stop by here tonight. He would understand this.*

Marianne giggled at something, which brought an icy stare from her father. She stopped, but it brought Peter back to attention.

"Certainly we see all Europe rising up under Hitler's tyranny," said Mr. Churchill from the radio. "What is now happening in Denmark is only one example. Let us then all go forward together, making the best of ourselves and the best of each other. . . ."

Everyone brightened at the mention of Denmark, but Peter wasn't quite sure what he had said just before that. At that point, the roar of German jamming slipped back into the broadcast, and though his Uncle Harald fiddled and fussed with the tuner some more, he could not bring back the English voice.

Finally Uncle Harald gave up and snapped off the set. "Well, that's that. At least we heard the part where he mentioned Denmark." A moment later, Uncle Harald left the room with Mikkel, and Aunt Hanne went to finish her cooking.

"Dinner in two minutes, Harald," she said. "Don't go too far." Then she looked at the four youngest, who were still sitting in the living room. "And you kids, are you ready for dinner? It's a little late tonight."

"We're ready, Mom," said Marianne. She started to get up, and Kurt cleared his throat.

"People of Denmark," he said in his best Churchill imitation, "we must fight this battle together."

Marianne threw a pillow from the sofa at him, but he just ducked.

"As I said, people of Denmark," he continued, "we must fight together, and we must find this lost British pilot. Your fearless leader, Kurt Ringsted, will lead you to the place where this unfortunate man is hiding."

Peter and Elise smiled as they got up from their chairs. But Peter wasn't smiling inside. To his cousin, everything seemed like a joke. But finding the pilot, bumping into German soldiers, and running into roadblocks only made him feel more and more tense, as if he wanted to scream or something. He wondered if Elise felt the same way.

STARTLING DISCOVERY

"We don't have enough bicycles to go around," Uncle Harald told them. "So we'll just walk to church this morning. It's been a while since we've done that, but it shouldn't take more than a half hour or so."

Everyone was dressed in their Sunday best. Elise had the summer dress her mother had sewn for her, and Peter had on his stiff white shirt. He didn't like wearing it much, but he couldn't wear his playclothes to church. Even Mikkel was scrubbed and dressed up.

The walk to town was actually a lot of fun; Uncle Harald told stories about finding lost sheep, and about the time that a ram butted him clear over the fence. Everyone laughed and tried to ignore the army trucks rolling by as they neared the outskirts of Ho. There seemed to be more of them than before, and more soldiers milling around than Peter remembered.

"They're still out looking for him," observed Mikkel. "It's Sunday morning, and they're still trying to find that pilot."

Aunt Hanne looked around with a worried expression. She checked with her husband, who nodded.

"I'm sure that's what it is," Uncle Harald told Mikkel. "It's been a full day now since that plane crashed. He had better find his way out of here soon."

Kurt gave Peter a wink and poked him in the ribs. Peter pretended not to notice.

"Let's try not to think about it now," interrupted Aunt Hanne. "This is Sunday, remember."

Inside the old church, Peter had plenty to look at as they waited for the service to start, and people came in quietly. Marianne, who was sitting to his left, pointed up at the ceiling, where the soaring white stucco walls turned into the beamed heights. It made Peter dizzy to look up at it.

Other than its unusual wooden steeple, the Ho church looked like a typical Danish church, with its red-tile roof and small rounded windows. It was old, maybe hundreds of years old, but there were older ones in other parts of the country. And it was smaller than many churches, but this was a small town after all.

Elise leaned over and whispered into Peter's ear. "There's Pastor Kai."

A man dressed in a black robe had slipped in through a side door in front and was mounting the steep steps to the high pulpit. The pulpit looked more like the crow's nest of a ship than a place from which the pastor would speak. Peter wondered how the man could stand wearing the ornamental pastor's collar; it looked as if someone had cut a hole just big enough for his neck in the middle of a small stack of paper plates. It was probably just as uncomfortable, too. But then the man cleared his throat and began to speak in his slow, easy way, and Peter quickly forgot about uncomfortable collars.

"I imagine everyone has heard what happened Friday night in Ho Bay." Pastor Kai scanned the faces of his congregation, a gathering of about fifty people. Most were farm families, Peter could tell, with a lot of older people but some with kids.

After a moment's hesitation, the pastor continued. "Many of us are deeply concerned and want to do anything we can to help . . . our friends. As I was thinking and praying about what this means to us, a lot comes to mind. We have been forced, in many cases, to help build the German fortresses and bunkers that line our beaches. It is a fact of war . . . and a sad chapter in our history.

"But there is still hope. There is still very much hope, and I have a good notion that this pilot—" He interrupted himself. "But let's go to the Bible to see how we might respond as Christians in such a situation. I can think of another time when something like this happened." He turned a few pages and started to read from the large pulpit Bible. It was the story of King David, before he was the king, and his best friend Jonathan.

"This is a familiar Old Testament story," continued the pastor, after he had read a few verses. "Our friend David is not yet the king, and he has been a very successful military man. But When King Saul sought after David's life, David's friend Jonathan had to make a hard decision. He knew where David was hiding. If he told, though, David would be killed. And there were those—especially the king, his own father—who would have wanted Jonathan to tell all." He rocked up on his heels, and his quiet voice raised a notch. "Now, would Jonathan betray his friend and obey the authorities, or would he do the right thing?"

There was a long pause, and Peter thought about a man, hiding for his life. For a second, he thought back to his friend Henrik again, the friend who had hidden in Peter's apartment last year. But the pastor was speaking about something else, and his gentle, pleading voice yanked Peter back to the present.

"What about us?" The man from the pulpit practically whispered the question.

Even Peter knew who the pastor was talking about. Not David or Jonathan, really. Peter was sure that everyone in the congregation knew this was a message for them, about the missing pilot. They seemed to hold their breath, and Peter did, too, as the pastor went on. Peter didn't remember understanding any pastor back home quite the way he understood Pastor Kai. This wasn't "preachy," the way he had heard people in church before. Twenty minutes went by, then a half hour, and Peter was still holding on to every word. He glanced over at Elise. She was on the edge of her seat, too.

Peter caught a movement out of the corner of his eye, and he glanced over at the back row. A crew-cut man, alone, was slipping out of the side aisle. Peter wasn't sure what, but something about the man made him look twice. Something far back in his mind told him he had seen the man before.

"Elise," he whispered in his sister's ear. "Look at the back row, quick. Where have we seen that guy before? The one who's leaving."

Elise looked over, too, but by then the man had disappeared. It left Peter with a strange feeling, but no one else seemed to notice the man.

Church was over in another ten minutes, leaving the Ringsteds, Elise, Peter, and the rest of the congregation to file out of church. Pastor Kai gave Peter a wink as he shook his hand. "See you in a little while, right?"

"Right," answered Peter. He was still thinking about the crew-cut man, trying to remember where he had seen him before. "Pastor?"

Pastor Kai was already shaking hands with the person behind Peter, an older woman, but he looked up. "Yes, Peter?"

"Did you see, um, did you see . . ." Suddenly Peter felt a little silly, not knowing if he should say anything about the man.

"Ah, never mind," Peter finished, shaking his head. He ran down the church front steps before the pastor could ask what he had meant. He didn't tell anyone else about what he had seen, but just listened to Kurt chattering in his usual way on the walk home.

"Wow," said Kurt. "I've never heard anything like that before. Pastor Kai was really hot this morning."

"I don't know about 'hot,' exactly," commented Aunt Hanne, "but there's no doubt he was direct about the matter, wasn't he?"

"He couldn't get into trouble for talking like that, could he?" asked Elise. "I think even the kids knew what he was talking about."

Aunt Hanne and Uncle Harald didn't say anything; they just looked at each other with a worried look.

"Pastor Kai does need to be careful, that's true." Uncle Harald shook his head. "Just like our own Mikkel."

The rest of the way home the two adults spoke only to each other, in voices too low for Peter and Elise to hear. The only thing they caught were the occasional stray words: *Mikkel. Underground. Too dangerous.* That was all Peter needed to hear.

———

Work waited for them at the farm. There was the bottle bum to feed and horse stalls to clean out. Peter and Elise volunteered to shovel the stalls, much to Kurt's amazement.

"Are you sure you want to do that?" asked Kurt. "You don't have to, you know."

"It's no problem," Peter insisted. "Really, we don't mind. Right, Elise?"

Elise shook her head no. "It's no problem," she agreed. "Really. Peter and I are a pretty good team."

"That's kind of you two," said Aunt Hanne. "Marianne, why don't you go with them? And Kurt, your father needs some help with the sheep. There are a few more hooves to trim."

For the next hour, Peter and Elise helped Marianne shovel the barn. It was hard work, and they took turns lugging the wheelbarrow. Peter, especially, threw himself into the work, trying not to think about anything else. Somehow it didn't seem like work. While Elise was out with a load, Peter paused on his shovel and looked around at the dark barn. Even though it smelled, he liked the barn, full of hay and plowing equipment. The two horses normally slept out in the field during the summer, just like the sheep, but they were allowed in at times.

He looked up at the rafters, and a bird fluttered. "Kind of reminds me of cleaning out my pigeon coop at home."

"Pigeons?" asked Marianne. "I didn't know you had pigeons. There are a few up in the barn, but they get in the way, Dad says."

Elise came rolling back in with the wheelbarrow just then. "They aren't just Peter's," she put in. "I have one, too, and so did Peter's friend Henrik, before we had to help him and his family escape to Sweden. They were Jews."

"Really? You really helped him escape?" asked Marianne, her eyes growing wide. "You never told us about that. That's scary."

"Yeah," Peter said quietly, turning away. He wasn't sure he wanted to get into all the details just then. Besides, someone was calling from the house for Marianne.

"Marianne? Are you out there?" It was Aunt Hanne. Marianne poked her head out of the door.

"Down here, Mom."

"Marianne, could you quit what you're doing and help me up here in the kitchen? The pastor and his family are coming down the driveway just now, and I'm not quite finished with dinner."

"Sure, Mom." Marianne leaned her shovel against the wall. Peter guessed it must have been two in the afternoon by then.

"Go ahead, Marianne," volunteered Elise. "We'll finish up here."

"Really? Thanks. Don't forget, though, you have to tell us your story soon." Marianne ran up the gravel path to the house, leaving Peter and Elise to finish. In a few minutes, they had another visitor to the barn.

"Haloo!" came a voice from the doorway. It was Pastor Kai's little boy, Jakob. "Can you play?"

"Sure," said Peter. "We were just playing 'Clean Out the Horse Barn.' You can play."

Little Jakob just giggled and rolled up his sleeves, then he started pitching handfuls of sweet-smelling hay onto the floor of the stall. He wasn't much help, but he definitely wasn't shy. While Peter and Elise filled up water troughs in the stalls, Jakob asked them about where they came from, how long it took to get here on the train, if they had any pets, and the names of their teachers at school.

"Has anyone ever told you you're a very curious little kid?" Peter asked, after Jakob finally ran out of questions for a moment.

"Sure," answered Jakob, with a big grin. "My dad and mom do all the time." The little blond boy seemed to take it as a compliment.

"So," continued Peter, when they had finished with the water. "Is there anything else you want to ask before we go back to the house?"

"Nope, nothing else." Jakob helped them put away their tools and parked the wheelbarrow. Then he stopped. "Okay, one thing. But my dad said not to ask you."

"Oh?" asked Peter. Now he was curious. "Why not?"

"I don't know," said Jakob, shrugging his shoulders. "He said *he* would."

"Oh, come on, Jakob," urged Peter. "What was he going to ask?"

Jakob hesitated, then threw up his hands. "Okay, but he said maybe you're not."

Peter took the little boy playfully by the shoulders. "You

don't say anything all the way, do you? Everything is just half-way. Maybe I'm not what?"

"He said maybe you aren't a Christian," said Jakob. He didn't even take a breath, and he looked up at Peter, without a fear. "So have you ever asked Jesus into your heart? I have, when I was little. It's easy. Have you?"

Coming from Jakob, the question was totally innocent. But for a minute, Peter felt as if his Uncle Morten was cornering him again, because his uncle had asked him the same thing last fall, only in a little different way. It made his head spin back then, and he didn't know what to say this time either. He let go of the little boy's shoulders as if they had given him an electric shock and took a step backward. He looked to Elise for help.

"I have, Jakob," she announced suddenly. "When I was about eight, I think, maybe just a little older than you are now, I prayed with my Uncle Morten to follow Jesus."

Peter stared at his sister. She had never mentioned anything like this to him, ever. Neither had his Uncle Morten.

"You did?" Peter asked her. "How come you never said anything to me about that?"

"I don't know," said Elise. She didn't look up but kicked hay around on the dirt floor. "I mean, I prayed and everything, but you know we don't go to church much, and none of my friends ever say anything about it."

"But I asked *Peter*," said Jakob. He wasn't ready for any confessions from anyone else, and like a hawk after a mouse, he would not be put off from his first question.

Peter fumbled for words, wishing the little blond preacher's kid would find something else to ask, something to distract him. He had been stung by the little boy's question, but he was glad his sister had stepped in. Still, what she had said about following Jesus made him wonder again. Everything was starting to fit together: The answered prayers. Rowing across to Sweden last fall. Finding the radio. And now his own sister. He had started to pray when the *big* troubles came, but it looked as if there was more to it than that. Maybe . . .

"Peter! Elise! Are you in here?" The barn door flew open and Marianne came running in. It took her a second for her eyes to adjust to the half-dark.

"Dad needs everybody's help. Three ewes are missing, and he can't figure out what happened to them. Somebody tore down a section of fence. He thinks they could be hurt."

Peter looked at Elise, then at Jakob. *Somebody tore it down?* "We better go help," he said. "We'll have to talk some more later, Jakob."

Marianne led the way outside, and they joined the others in the fields, looking under heather, around bushes, and behind trees, calling for the missing sheep. Even Pastor Kai was there, beating the brush with a long stick and whistling. Little Jakob ran around from person to person, getting in the way. Everyone forgot about dinner.

"How can you tell if any are missing, anyway?" Peter asked Kurt as they hiked through a hilly section of heather. This part of the farm was bogs, bushes, meadows, and small woods— hundreds of places for sheep to get lost or hurt. Kurt knew most of the hiding places, so Elise and Peter stayed close by.

"We count," explained Kurt. "It's easy. Mostly they stick together, but sometimes they get themselves lost, they get their foot caught or something, and then they just sit there. That's probably all that happened. You should see them if they get flipped onto their backs. They just lie there like a turtle with all fours up in the air, and they can't move. They're not too bright. It usually happens way out of the way, like in a bog or something."

"Like that kind of bog?" asked Elise. She pointed to a low spot, covered by heather and bushes and thick brambles. They turned aside, and Peter pulled back a branch. No sheep there.

On the other side of the bog, a few paces away, Elise saw something else. Everyone heard her gasp.

"What, what?" Peter stepped over to see what she saw. "There's nothing in there. You see something?"

"A leg!" She yelled, in a way Peter had never heard her yell before. "There's a real leg in there! Uncle Harald!"

Pastor Kai was the first to come running; Uncle Harald must have been too far off to hear. The kids clustered around behind him, like chicks behind the mother hen. Peter peeked to see if there was anything attached to the leg, and there was—a body; someone in a torn uniform hidden under a thick mat of bushes. It was hard to tell, covered with mud, but this was certainly not a German. The man's face was scraped badly, and all Peter could see of his skin was bruised beyond belief. Peter winced.

"Is it the Englander, Daddy?" Jakob was the first to say anything. "Is he alive?"

Pastor Kai wheeled around. "Jakob! You need to go back to the Ringsted farm, right now." He looked over at Marianne. "Marianne, please take him back, would you? In fact, all you kids, run back to the house, right now. You don't need to see this. Kurt, where's your father?"

"I don't know, Pastor Kai." Kurt looked around. "But I see Mikkel over there."

"Good," said the pastor. "Get him for me, will you? Hurry!"

Kurt jumped up and ran toward his brother while everyone else froze in fear.

"Come on, kids, get going!" barked the pastor. They weren't used to hearing Pastor Kai sound like a drill sergeant. The man on the ground groaned softly, and everyone jumped.

Elise gasped again. "He's alive!"

Pastor Kai looked down. "He may be, friends, but he won't be as long as we stand here staring at him lying in the mud like this. Come on! Oh, and Marianne—" He grabbed her arm as she turned. "You need to have your mother fix up a bed for this fellow. Then call Doctor Knudsen as quickly as you can and have him meet us at your home. But whatever you do, do not tell him yet who we've found, do you understand? It's enough to say a guest of your father is injured and needs help right away. Do you understand?"

Marianne nodded and took Jakob's hand. "Come on, Jakob." She dragged him down the path.

Back at the house, Peter and Elise felt as if they were in the middle of another wild rescue operation, almost like the first night they had arrived at the farm. Marianne laid out another bed with extra sheets, and pulled out supplies to clean the injured man while Aunt Hanne tried desperately to reach the doctor on the phone.

"What do you mean, he's out at the Elleman place?" Her voice had an edge to it. "They don't have a phone, do they? Yes, well, I don't know, exactly, it's just that I'd like to speak with him myself. No, no message. We'll get in touch with him ourselves. Thank you."

Aunt Hanne looked straight at Kurt. "Kurt, this is important." Kurt nodded. "Get on your bicycle and bring word to Doctor Knudsen. He's over at the Elleman farm, on the other side of town, checking in on old Mrs. Elleman. Heaven knows why they don't have a telephone. This is 1944, after all. She's probably talking his ear off about her aches and pains. Just get over there quickly and bring him back. And where is your father?"

She looked out the window, searching the field beyond. Her husband was nowhere to be seen.

"Okay, Mom," Kurt assured her. "Come on, Peter."

In a minute, the two boys were on their bicycles, racing as fast as their legs would move them, bumping over potholes and jumping over ruts. By that time, both boys had figured out that Peter was the faster rider, but Kurt did his best, and they rode side by side.

"How far, Kurt?" yelled Peter.

"Fifteen minutes, tops. Down this road, past town, then it's the second farm on the left." Kurt looked over at Peter, and the race was on. But it wasn't long before Kurt started to lag behind, and finally he stopped. Peter looked back.

"Are you okay?" asked Peter.

"I—I think so," answered Kurt. But he made a terrible face, and he was breathing hard.

"You just have to go ahead," puffed Kurt. "My side is killing me." Peter realized Kurt wasn't kidding. "I'll catch up in a ... minute. You go ahead."

Peter hesitated. "Me?"

"Yes, you, Peter. You're faster than I am, and I told you already where the place is."

"Okay, okay." Peter repeated the directions Kurt had given him. "Through town, past the road to Bluewater Hook, and then the second farm on the left. What happens if the doctor's not there?"

"He's there. Go on, you have to hurry!"

"Second farm on the left," Peter said, hesitating. "What's the name again? Entenman?"

"Elleman," said Kurt, pushing on the back of Peter's bicycle.

There was no time to argue about it. Peter tried not to think about losing his way or not being able to find the farm. He just put his head down and pedaled—through the small patches of woods, past the parsonage and the church, down the small village main street, past the large Ho Inn, and out of town again. He looked up then, studying the fields outside town.

"There's the first place," he counted as he raced past farm number one. The second farm came up in a moment, so he pulled down the short lane leading to the whitewashed square building. Another bicycle, a large black one, was leaning against the house, and Peter pounded on the heavy front door.

"Hello, Doctor, Doctor—" Just then Peter couldn't remember

the name of the man he was sent for, and he bit his tongue trying to remember. To make up for his forgetfulness, he pounded on the door a bit harder. No answer. He ran around the side, then heard the door opening and ran back again. A kindly-looking, middle-aged man was standing there, looking out at the front yard.

"I'm looking for the doctor," said Peter, coming around the corner of the house.

"Then you've found him." The man smiled. "I'm Doctor Knudsen." He squinted at Peter, who was standing there, feeling awkward. "You're the Ringsted's nephew, right?"

Small town, thought Peter. *Everybody knows me, but I don't know them.* He nodded. "I'm Peter, and I'm supposed to ask if you can come out to the farm right away. Can you?"

"Well, yes, I'm finished here with Mrs. Elleman, I suppose. What's the problem?"

"Pastor Kai said—I mean, my uncle has a visitor with a problem. He just needs to see you right away. It's an emergency."

The doctor frowned, not quite understanding. "Pastor Kai is out there with you? He's sick?"

"No, no, it's not Pastor Kai. He's there, but he's not the one who needs you."

"Then who needs me, young man?"

This was getting ridiculous, thought Peter. He wished the doctor would just get on his bicycle and come to the farm with him. He didn't know how to answer the man's questions without telling him the whole story.

"I don't know his name, Doctor Knudsen. All I know is that this man is hurt bad."

The doctor shook his head but disappeared into the house to get his bag. In a minute, he returned, strapped his bag on the back of his large black bicycle, and pedaled off. Peter struggled to keep up. Halfway there, they met Kurt, coming toward them. Peter's cousin made a quick U-turn.

"That was quick!" said Kurt. It had been less than fifteen minutes, Peter guessed. "You found him okay."

"He found me," said the doctor. "But this odd cousin of yours can't tell me who is sick, or hurt, only that I need to get there right away. Can you tell me what's going on, or do I need to ask your father?"

"Well," said Kurt, looking over at Peter. "It's kind of a long story. I think maybe my dad can explain it better than I can."

Peter thought Kurt was being especially careful, but he felt foolish for not being able to tell the doctor exactly what was going on. It was only a few more minutes of riding, though, and they pulled into the Ringsted drive. Uncle Harald was struggling up the driveway toward the house with a young sheep over his shoulders, and he turned around when he heard the doctor call his name.

"Harald," said the doctor. "Finally someone who can tell me what's going on here."

"What's that?" asked Uncle Harald. "I'll tell you what's going on. This one broke its leg, two others killed. I had to use a tin can to wrap the leg still. Some idiot pulled down a piece of our fence and put their dog on the animals. I finally found her way over at the edge of the property." Then he looked at the doctor with a puzzled expression. "What can I do for you, Finn?"

"That's what I'd like to know," replied the doctor, looking as puzzled as Uncle Harald. "I'm sorry to hear about your animals, but your young nephew came racing over to find me. All he could say was that someone was hurt."

Uncle Harald looked at Peter again, and he was just as puzzled as the doctor. "Who's hurt, Peter?"

It was then that Pastor Kai leaned out the window nearest to the front door. He motioned at Doctor Knudsen, calling him over. "Doctor, I'm glad to see you. In here, please." Then he disappeared into the house again. Uncle Harald looked at the doctor, gently put down the injured ewe, and followed him inside. He looked back through the doorway at Kurt.

"Son, put this animal in the barn, would you, while I see what's going on here."

Peter followed his uncle inside. It took only one look for the doctor to understand who his patient was and what had happened. The man was lying on the guest bed, and someone had cleaned him up a bit. Still, Peter thought the man looked barely alive, and with more bruises than he had ever seen on anyone. His whole face was black and puffy.

Everyone crowded around the door of the room or tried to peek inside, waiting for what the doctor would say. The room was hushed for a time, and Doctor Knudsen mumbled to himself as he checked the pilot. He carefully examined the man's head, checking ears and eyes.

"No broken bones," he finally said. "But there are plenty of scrapes and bruises. And it looks like he got a pretty good blow to the head. Concussion." He prepared a bandage and looked over at Aunt Hanne. "I can't tell how serious, though. Has he said anything since you found him, or has he moved?"

"All he's done is groaned a couple of times," said Aunt Hanne, "and he's moved a little since we got him here."

"Hanne," interrupted Uncle Harald. "You're going to have to explain to me how this man got here."

"The kids found him, Harald," answered Pastor Kai. "He appears to be the British pilot who crash-landed in the bay the other night."

"What's a percussion, doctor?" interrupted Kurt, who had stepped in from the barn.

"*Concussion*," corrected Doctor Knudsen. "The shock of being hit on the head causes brain tissue to swell. That can mean anything from a simple headache to death. Fortunately, there's no sign of anything more serious, like a hematoma. It's hard to tell, though. He really should be in a hospital, but considering who he is, I'm afraid that would be a trifle difficult. I'd feel much better if he regained consciousness."

As if on cue, the man on the bed stirred and tried to say something.

"That's what he's been doing," said Aunt Hanne.

"What did he say?" asked Marianne, who was standing next to the bed with a washrag and a basin.

"Sounded like, 'Old One, Drummer,' " Kurt guessed.

"No, Kurt, it was 'Hold on, gunner,' " said Peter. It was hard to tell.

While they were guessing, the pilot's eyelids fluttered, just as the doctor had hoped.

"Look at his eyes!" Marianne pointed at the man. She had been gently dabbing at his bruised face with the washrag.

The doctor looked more closely at his patient. "I think he's coming around—" But before Dr. Knudsen had finished his sentence, the pilot's eyes popped open, and he raised his hands as if to fend off a blow. He looked up at the doctor, with his eyes wide, and the kids all stepped back, not knowing what to expect.

"Sprechen Sie Englisch?" the man asked in German. (Which means, "Do you speak English?")

"My German is pretty rusty," replied the doctor in English, "but I'm a doctor. You hold still."

The injured pilot forced a small smile, behind all the bruises. "You're Danish, correct?"

"That's right," answered the doctor. "I'm Doctor Finn Knudsen, and you're at the Ringsted sheep farm."

The man tried to lift himself up, but the doctor put a hand on his shoulder. "I said you must not move," repeated Dr. Knudsen. "You've had a nasty blow to the head—a concussion—and right now you need to stay completely still. I'm glad you're awake, though. You must have been out for quite some time."

"Off and on, actually," said the pilot. He closed his eyes in pain. "How long has it been?"

"You crashed Friday night, and now it's Sunday afternoon," the doctor told him. "Do you know what has happened to you?"

The pilot closed his eyes. "It must have been a lucky shot," he said, barely moving his lips. "I can't remember anything after we ditched in the bay. But where's Skeffington? Have you seen my gunner?"

Dr. Knudsen put his hand on the man's shoulder once more, and everyone looked at Mikkel, who had just arrived out in the hall. He made his way to the bed.

"I'm Mikkel," he introduced himself, "and I'm making sure your radio gets to the right people."

The pilot opened his eyes and gave him a knowing look. "I see. I am Thomas Whitbread, Captain, Royal Air Force. I shall be out and away at my earliest opportunity, I assure you."

The man tried to raise his head, but fell back in pain.

The doctor pulled out a stethoscope and gently placed the metal disk on Captain Whitbread's chest. "You're not going to move until I say you can move, my dear captain. You must have been wandering around in a daze just after you crashed. I surely cannot tell you why you didn't wander into the hands of the Germans who were searching for you, or how you happened to hide yourself the way you did. My friend the pastor here would agree that someone was watching over you, most certainly."

Peter looked at the injured man, then at Mikkel, then at the doctor. By the way Mikkel was talking, he obviously felt safe around Doctor Knudsen.

"Captain?" asked Mikkel. "When it's time, we'll get you out of here. I promise. Captain?"

But Captain Whitbread had closed his eyes again and looked as if he had drifted off to an uneasy sleep. Then his eyes fluttered for a moment. "You never told me what happened to my gunner."

Everyone looked at Mikkel again, who took a deep breath. "I . . . we went out to the plane just after you crashed, but you had already escaped. I don't know how you moved so fast. Your gunner, I'm sorry, he's dead. I'm very sorry."

The pilot sighed deeply, not opening his eyes. "Skeffington," he whispered. "Maybe, maybe I knew that, but I don't seem to recall. Skeffington." He looked as if he would cry, then seemed to catch himself. "I'm sorry, too."

In the uneasy silence that followed, Kurt pulled Peter and Elise back into the hall, and Marianne followed. "I've got a plan," he whispered.

"What are you talking about?" Peter whispered back.

"You know. For getting the captain out of here and back to England. We can do it."

"Kurt," said Marianne, "this man just heard about his friend being killed, and you're talking about plans? What's wrong with you?"

Kurt rubbed his forehead and looked at his sister with a pained expression. "I know, Marianne. But we can do something. Don't you think?"

Just then Mikkel shuffled out of the guest room and started walking down the hall. He glanced over at Kurt and gave him a suspicious look. "You leave this guy alone, Kurt," said Mikkel. "He needs to get better as soon as he can."

"I know." Kurt didn't hesitate.

"And don't say a word of this to anyone, not even your best friend, understand?"

"Right, not even to my best friend," echoed Kurt. As Mikkel continued back down the hall, Kurt turned to look at Peter and Elise again. "I'll tell you about the plan later," he whispered.

Peter wished his cousin would just forget about it, but as the long afternoon turned into evening, there seemed little chance of that. Peter tried to help with the captain, but there was nothing he could do, really. He and Elise ended up in the kitchen, and they volunteered to do dinner dishes.

"You would never offer to do this at home," Elise said to her brother.

"Neither would you," he replied.

Elise just shrugged, and Peter understood. He felt the need to be doing something, too. Anything. Marianne was helping her mother and Mrs. Steffensen, and Kurt was out with his father taking care of the ewe that had been attacked by the dog. Peter didn't know where Mikkel or the pastor had gone to. Little Jakob was playing quietly in the living room.

Elise cleared the dishes from their hurried meal, and Peter heated up water on the stove. Dinner with the pastor and his family had not turned out the way they had expected. Everyone was jumping up and down like nervous sheep, taking care of the captain. Peter was scraping another dish when he heard voices outside the kitchen window.

"Honestly, Mikkel, I appreciate your judgment, but how can you be sure about something like this?" The voice was Pastor Kai's. Peter recognized Mikkel's voice, too, but couldn't make out all his words. It made him feel slightly guilty, but he couldn't help hearing the conversation as it drifted in. He looked over at Elise, who was piling dirty plates on the counter.

"Should we be hearing that?" Peter asked her quietly.

"Hearing what?"

Peter pointed his thumb in the direction of the voices.

"My sermons would cause them to think that?" continued Pastor Kai. "That's a bit difficult to accept."

Then Mikkel's sharp voice came in louder through the window as he became more serious. "I'm telling you, pastor, I saw the list, and everyone the Germans have ever put on that list have either disappeared or been shot. What you said this morning didn't help matters. It's that simple."

"But why?" asked the pastor. "There must be a mistake."

"Mistake or not, Pastor, you've got to admit your sermons have been pretty fiery lately. The Nazis keep track of people who say things against them, you know, even in out of the way little towns like Ho and Oksby. Nobody gets away with saying the kinds of things you've been saying. Not for very long."

"So what are you saying to me?"

"I'm saying you're in danger, that you need to take a long vacation somewhere where they only speak either Swedish or English. I know people who can get you out of here, and that's what you need to do. You need to get out of here soon and take your family with you. It's for your own safety."

"Well, yes, Mikkel, as I said, I very much appreciate your concern, and I will think about this seri—"

"I'm sorry, Pastor, but thinking about this is not good enough. This pilot is not the only one whose life is in danger now." Mikkel's voice trailed off then, and he must have walked off, leaving the pastor alone outside. Peter and Elise just stared at each other. Peter didn't know what to think. *Pastor Kai! His life's in danger?* It made Peter feel helpless to hear what he had just heard and not know what to do about it.

"Should we tell anyone?" Peter half whispered to Elise, who had put down her dishes.

"I don't think so," Elise replied. "It's not our business."

When he pushed through the back door, Pastor Kai looked startled to see Peter and Elise standing in the kitchen. Both of them stared at him, wondering if he knew they had heard. But he only smiled his usual big smile.

"You look as if you could use some help with the dishes," he said, rolling up his sleeves. "Here, let me help you a little bit before we have to leave."

It didn't take long; about ten minutes later the women came back into the kitchen from the bedroom where Captain Whitbread was.

"I think he's comfortable now, at least," announced Mrs. Steffensen. She noticed her husband up to his elbows in soapsuds. "Making yourself useful, dear?"

"Yes, as a matter of fact," replied the pastor. "But it really is time to be leaving."

He wiped his soapy hands off on a dish towel. Aunt Hanne, who had come in with a load of bedding in her arms, looked worried.

"I'm so terribly sorry for everything we've put you through here today," she said. "This was supposed to have been a pleasant, relaxing dinner."

The pastor just smiled, and his wife put her hand on Aunt Hanne's shoulder. Little Jakob came and stood close to his mother, being especially quiet.

"I'm very glad we were here," said the pastor. Mrs. Steffensen nodded in agreement. "Now we just have to find a safe place for our captain friend. I understand the Germans have already been by once, searching for him here in the house."

As Uncle Harald and Kurt came back from the barn, everyone said their goodbyes and thank-yous. The Steffensens got on their bicycles, and Pastor Kai snapped his finger as if remembering something. He turned around.

"Shame on us for almost forgetting," he told Kurt. "Happy eleventh birthday in advance! Your day is on Monday, isn't it?"

Kurt beamed. "No, it's the day after tomorrow. Tuesday. My cousins are going to help me celebrate."

The day after tomorrow? thought Peter, glancing at Elise. No one had told them. They would have to think of a quick present!

Code Name Dagmar

"Come on, Peter and Elise, you have to see this!" Kurt tugged at Peter's sleeve, pulling him away from the breakfast table.

"After breakfast dishes, Mr. Ringsted," said Aunt Hanne, in a half-serious tone that still meant business. "Your turn this week, remember?"

"Mom!" protested Kurt. "I just have to show them something."

"Oh, Mom, nothing," responded his mother. "All you have to clean up are a few bowls from the oatmeal."

Everyone ended up pitching in to finish the dishes, and then Peter, Elise, and Marianne followed Kurt out to the barn section of the house, the part that was attached. At one time, animals had been kept there, but now it was mainly a workshop and storage area. Uncle Harald and Mikkel were already out there, clearing off a section of the floor, pushing aside plows and bags of fertilizer. Then Uncle Harald reached down, put his finger into what looked like a small knothole, and tugged. Nothing happened.

"You can tell we haven't been in this root cellar in several months." Uncle Harald grunted and tried to lift the stubborn door again.

"Here, Dad," said Mikkel, jumping to his side. "Let me help." He found a broken handle from a hoe, and they put it in the finger hold. With both of them pulling and grunting, the door finally cracked open with a protesting squeak.

"Wow!" cried Peter, as the door was opened to uncover a small, dark root cellar. Mikkel clicked on a flashlight to reveal a dusty cave about the size of a large closet. Floor to ceiling shelves held empty glass canning jars.

Uncle Harald peered down inside. "Here, let's clean this out a bit."

Taking turns down in the hole, Peter and Kurt passed up jars to the others. They swept out the hard dirt floor and pulled out splintered boards. There was even a rusty piece of machinery that Peter guessed had once been part of a truck or a tractor.

"You look like one of those actors who paint their faces." Elise had to laugh as she took an armload of scrap wood from her brother. Everyone else looked and laughed, too.

"Just call me a coal miner," said Peter. It felt good to laugh, even for a minute.

"Well, at least this gives us a good excuse to clean up that old cellar," observed Uncle Harald. "Your aunt has been after me for months about it."

Next they lowered a small table with a kerosene lamp, several blankets, and a fresh layer of hay. It would be cramped for the Englishman, but at least it would be comfortable. Kurt looked over the edge.

"Hey, Dad, can I stay down there? It looks like a great room."

"Sorry, son," replied his father. "There's only enough space for one."

And it was barely big enough for the captain to stretch out after they had lowered him down into it. Still, it was a perfect hiding room. He still couldn't raise his head without feeling ill, and Peter thought the man looked quite helpless, lying on his cot.

"I'm very sorry we must put you in such a room," apologized Aunt Hanne in her broken English. She had already apologized several times about the arrangement, but the captain just waved his hand.

"It's quite comfortable, actually." He brushed off the apology, closing his eyes and touching his bandaged head. "I am the one who is sorry to put you into this kind of danger. . . ." He looked as if he were dropping off to sleep again. "As soon as we make contact, I'll be out of here. . . ."

Then Mikkel piped up. "It's only until we make radio contact with London and arrange for someone to come pick you up. Just a few days, I'm sure."

The pilot didn't hear him, or didn't move, and Aunt Hanne motioned for everyone to leave the man alone.

"Hey, Mikkel, can we watch you set up the radio?" asked Kurt as everyone started leaving to finish their morning chores.

"Who said I still had the radio?" Mikkel asked back. He looked around at his audience: Kurt, Marianne, Peter, and Elise, and he sighed. "I wish I didn't. But some guys in Esbjerg are waiting for it, and I haven't been able to move it around to a safer place yet. The Nazis are everywhere out on the roads."

"And they're still looking for Captain Whitbread, right?" asked Peter.

"Right. Only, they don't know that's who they're looking for." Mikkel smiled for the first time. "Well, I don't know why I'm doing this, but come on." He motioned for the four to follow him, and they walked over to a portion of the barn where Uncle Harald had set up his workshop. There were bits of machinery scattered about, things like broken water pumps, plow blades, and hay balers. But the worktable itself was neatly arranged with hand tools hanging in rows. Mikkel reached under the table and felt for something.

"What are you doing?" asked Kurt impatiently.

"Just a minute; I said I would show you." Mikkel took hold of a small wooden box, something that looked like it might hold a shirt rather than a secret radio. But there was no shirt. Peter and Elise stared as Mikkel carefully set the box down on the table, opened up the hinged top, and pulled out the radio. It was only the size of a cigar box and was filled with wires, switches, and glass cylinders that looked like sausage-shaped light bulbs.

Peter pointed at the contraption and moved in closer for a better look. He had never seen a two-way radio before. "Wow, what are all those things in there?" he asked.

"Careful," replied Mikkel. "Don't touch anything. Those are tubes, and they can break." He connected a Morse code keyboard that looked like a small switch with a handle, and the earphones. Then he pulled down a coil of wire from the workbench. "Here's the antenna. One of you run it out the door and attach it to the highest tree you can find. It's better at night, but we can give it a try."

"We will!" Kurt was eager to help. He and Peter unrolled the wire slowly as they backed out the door. A young oak tree just outside was far enough away to loop the end of the wire over.

Back inside, Mikkel had wired the radio up to a large battery under the workbench, and he was ready to turn it on. He even had a small pad and paper.

"Come on, Mikkel, let's see!" Kurt jumped up and down. Peter was interested, too, but he tried not to show it.

"Keep your shirt on," said Mikkel, fiddling with a dial. "And remember, this radio doesn't have a speaker. Now hold the noise down while I see if we can get through."

Everyone kept silent while Mikkel worked the Morse code key. He made it click to a woodpecker rhythm, and Peter tried to pick out any letters he knew. There was one—"S" was three short clicks. He thought he heard another—"V," which was three short, followed by one long. Dit-dit-dit-dah. But everything went too fast for him, and the clicks blended together. After a few minutes, the others were starting to lose interest. But he could tell by Mikkel's expression that his older cousin was somewhere else.

"Hear anything?" whispered Peter.

"Shh," replied Mikkel. "Yeah, I think I'm getting through to London this time!"

There was a pause, while Mikkel scribbled furiously on the pad. Everyone crowded around to see the message.

"Ack Whtbrd safe," repeated Marianne, though they could all read what was written. Mikkel raised his left finger to his lips.

"Shh, I can't hear," he whispered. They waited for what seemed like five minutes, maybe ten, while Mikkel waited for the rest of his message.

After a time, Mikkel started writing again. Peter read the rest of the message to himself: *Sub arrive 55–33–30, 8–12E, time code name Dagmar.* It didn't make much sense, except the "sub arrive" part, but he was afraid to say anything until Mikkel was done. His cousin put down the pencil, tapped out a ten-second reply, and pulled off his headphones.

"That was it?" asked Kurt, looking disappointed.

"That was it," said Mikkel as he folded up his equipment. "We just spoke, I mean communicated with the Defense Ministry in London, England. They knew exactly who we were talking about."

"So what's the message mean?" asked Marianne.

Mikkel pointed to the paper where he had written the message. " 'Ack Whtbrd safe' just means they acknowledge that Whitbread is safe. You know, they understand he's okay. Then the other part, the part that took a little longer, is where they said how they're going to pick him up."

"All that, in just a few words?" asked Elise.

"Sure," explained Mikkel. Even though Mikkel talked tough a lot of the time, Peter thought he was enjoying some of the attention just then. " 'Sub arrive 55–33–30, 8–12E' means a submarine is going to pick him up. He must be pretty important. And '55–33–30' is the spot on the coast. You know, fifty-five degrees, thirty-three minutes, thirty seconds is the exact spot on the Danish coast, the latitude. Eight degrees, twelve minutes is how far away from England, and 'E' is for east. I'm going to have to look it up on the map, but I'm sure it's close to a beach nearby, one that's not mined. I told them where we're located, too."

Mikkel explained the numbers and degrees part too quickly for Peter to follow, but he already knew degrees meant how far apart things were.

"And then, 'time code name Dagmar' just means that we have to listen to the BBC to hear when our pick-up time is."

"The BBC?" asked Kurt. "Are you kidding?"

"No, really," Mikkel assured him. "You know, at the end of the broadcast, when they say things like, 'Greetings to Hans in Copenhagen'?"

"Sure, but I just thought—"

"Well, those are all messages to the Underground, code names, times when they're going to drop weapons, all that. That's one reason why the Germans are always trying to block the signal. You didn't know that?"

Kurt shrugged. "How should I know that?"

Peter hadn't known, either, but he was learning. He wasn't sure he wanted to, but he was learning.

Then Marianne brightened, as if she had just come up with the answer to a math problem. "Oh, I get it," she announced. "So when we hear on the radio that Dagmar is coming—like on Monday at nine—we know that's when they can pick up the captain."

"Almost," replied Mikkel. "The message is going to be more like, 'Greetings to Dagmar, who will celebrate her birthday this

Friday night at nine.' Something like that."

"Neat!" Kurt brightened, then he wrinkled his nose. "But why don't they just call you up on this radio again?"

Mikkel chuckled. "They would, and they probably will, but I'm not the regular contact. They might not get through, and besides, the radio has to go to someone else as soon as I can get it to them. Giving the message over the BBC is just a safe way to make sure we get the word." Then he frowned. "As long as the Germans don't jam it."

Everyone seemed satisfied with Mikkel's explanation, but Peter still wondered, thinking of the Germans who were searching with their dogs, and the man they were now hiding. Would Dagmar's birthday come in time, before anyone else found out?

8

OUT OF CONTROL

By Tuesday morning, Peter and Elise were getting used to the farm routine. Up at five-thirty, chores outside until seven, in for breakfast. After breakfast, there were still more chores, and then usually the four kids had some time for exploring or riding their bikes. But this morning was a little different.

Happy Birthday, Kurt. Peter didn't say it out loud, but he was the first one out of bed. He slipped on some clothes in the morning light, picked up a book from the small bedside table, and tiptoed out the bedroom door.

The book, called *A Hunt for Adventure*, was about four boys who built a fort, and a raft, and had all sorts of adventures. He had brought it from home, thinking he would have time to read during the summer. As it was, he had been mostly too busy with his own adventures, even though he had liked the book so far. When Peter reached the door to the girls' room, he tapped lightly three times.

"Elise," he whispered, "are you awake?"

No one answered.

"Elise?"

He cracked open the door, and Elise rolled over in her bed to look up at him. She blinked her eyes.

"Is it time to get up already?" she mumbled and scratched her nose.

Peter put his finger to his lips. "I just thought of something we could give Kurt for his birthday."

"Oh." She buried her face in her pillow, burrowing her itchy nose. "Is that what you're waking me up for?"

"Yeah. We can give him my book. All you have to do is write in the front." Peter held it out in front of his sister, with a pencil.

"Why do you want to give away your book?" Elise asked sleepily.

"Because he'll like it. Kurt even asked me if he could read it when I was done. I can't think of anything else we could give him."

Elise was quiet for a moment. "Okay, I can't either." She took the pencil Peter gave her and wrote her name on the opening page, under her brother's. She tried to focus her eyes on what her brother had already written. He recited it for her.

"It says 'Happy Birthday and best wishes from your cousins, Peter and Elise,' and then the date, 11 July, 1944. How's that?"

"Terrific," she replied through the pillow.

———

Now Peter and Elise were prepared for the party. As soon as they all came back in from their morning chore of feeding the Ringsteds' chickens, Elise got some brown wrapping paper from her aunt. She wrapped the present while Aunt Hanne decorated the breakfast table with candles and two miniature Danish flags.

"It looks to me like someone is having a party," boomed their uncle, pushing through the door with a smile. "Who might that be?"

No one needed to answer. When Kurt followed his father in a moment later, everyone sang the Danish birthday song: "To-day it is Kurt's birth-day, hurra, hurra, hurra!" Their uncle's deep voice drowned out everyone else's, and it was slightly off-key, but it didn't seem to matter. Kurt beamed, everyone clapped, and Aunt Hanne poured steaming oatmeal into everyone's bowl. Then Marianne got up, as if to make a speech.

"Time to open presents!" She waved at a small package sitting on the table.

Peter pulled their book out from where he had been hiding it in his lap and offered it to his cousin. "Here, Kurt, this is from Elise and me."

Kurt tore the wrapping off the book and held it up with a smile. "Hey, great," he said. "You knew I wanted to read this. Thanks!"

Marianne and her mother each gave Kurt a pair of socks they had knitted. Kurt wasn't as enthusiastic about that, but he was polite. Then everyone looked at Uncle Harald as he cleared his throat.

"Well, young man," he began, "I think now that you're eleven, you're old enough for some additional responsibility. You're old enough to handle a pair of reins." With that, he reached under his chair, pulled out a pair of leather reins, and tossed them on top of the small pile of wrapping paper in front of Kurt.

For a moment, Kurt stared at the reins in front of him. His grin turned to a puzzled expression, but Uncle Harald said nothing else.

"Um, I don't think I get it," said Kurt. "Does this mean . . . What *does* this mean?"

His father laughed and looked at Aunt Hanne. She passed back the smile.

"This is a kind of treasure hunt," explained Uncle Harald.

"You're just going to have to find out what these reins go to, and then that's your present."

Kurt's eyes lit up as he finally started to understand. "Oh, now I get it. Like a horse or something!"

"Or something," answered his dad. "But go on out to the barn and find out."

Kurt led the way to the attached barn, while everyone followed close behind. The first place Kurt checked was down in the root cellar, where the captain was lying on his cot.

"Birthday?" asked the captain, hiding a grin. "No one told me about any birthday." He looked up at Peter and winked. But even Peter didn't know what the present was, or where it was hidden.

Peter looked over at his uncle, who waved his hand at Aunt Hanne. She disappeared behind a tall stack of wooden boxes, only to reappear a moment later pulling a small, two-wheeled cart, something like a miniature horse-racing cart. It was painted bright red and draped with streamers. The two wheels had been salvaged from old bicycles, and the body looked very much like an old wheelbarrow, but there was no mistaking what it was: A goat cart!

Kurt saw it as soon as he came up the ladder from the cellar. He ran over and sat down in it. "This is terrific! Better than a bike, even."

"Well, now, Kurt, it's just to play around in," warned his mother. "You don't want to overburden the animals. You're almost too big for this, but your father thought it would be fun. I think he wishes he were your size, so he could ride in it."

"Oh, Kurt's not too big," said Mikkel. He had just come in from outside, leading one of their largest goats. "Here, let's try this one on for size."

It took only a minute for Mikkel and Uncle Harald to strap the reluctant animal between the two poles attached to the cart, and then to string around the reins for Kurt to hold. The goat threw his white head back, as if to shake the feeling of a harness, something he had not worn before. Even Peter could tell this was going to take some getting used to. As soon as they let go, Kurt was off, and the goat started running this way and that, all over the courtyard. The reins seemed to have little or no effect on the animal. Everyone cheered, while Marianne ran after her brother with a cone-shaped party hat.

"You have to wear this," she shouted.

Marianne managed to catch the cart and hold the goat back just long enough for Kurt to get his party hat on. And then he was off once more. Everyone followed him around to the back of the house, laughing hysterically at Kurt bumping over the path, almost upsetting the cart.

"Here now," announced Mikkel. "We'll have to have some birthday races. Kurt in the cart with the goat, against everyone else, running." He pointed to a large tree. "From here to the tree and back. Ready?"

Kurt was trying to get control of the goat, pulling it this way and that. The goat was proving that she was more than strong enough to pull a boy like Kurt. The only question was, which way?

Kurt struggled with his reins, still trying to turn the animal. "No! Wait a minute! I'm not ready."

"Go!" Mikkel wasn't listening to his brother, and everyone was off running.

Halfway to the tree, Peter felt something yank his pants from the back belt loop, and he was thrown off balance. He stumbled, and Elise shot past him. But he only laughed and picked himself up again.

"You're going to wish you hadn't done that!" he yelled at his sister.

"Only if you catch me." Elise was now ahead by several steps and almost to the old tree. Mikkel was running backwards, and Aunt Hanne was even pulling Uncle Harald along by the arm.

Everyone was laughing, mostly at the sight of Kurt in his new little goat cart, going in circles.

Elise ended up winning the race, while everyone behind her shouted and laughed.

"She cheated," protested Peter, trying his best to look serious. "She held me back."

Uncle Harald patted Peter on the head and clucked his tongue in pretend sympathy. Elise only strutted by and grinned straight into Peter's face, almost rubbing noses. Peter tried to tweak her nose with his fingers, which sent her running. Kurt was still going in circles.

"Hey, Peter!" yelled Kurt from the cart. "Why don't you try and see if you can get this crazy animal to go in a straight line?"

Peter was eager to try. "Sure!" Kurt bailed out of his seat and held the goat while Peter got on.

"Hey!" Mikkel suddenly yelled. "Did somebody leave the gate to the ram pasture open?"

Peter looked over at the pasture where Uncle Harald kept five or six of the aggressive rams just in time to see a large ram head out through an opening in the fence and disappear around the front of the house.

Marianne and Kurt had told them stories about the rams, about how people had been cornered in the barns for hours by the animals, and how, left to themselves, they would act like the meanest watchdogs, charging anyone who got in their way. Everyone, especially Peter and Elise, stayed away from the ram pasture. Mikkel set off running to get the gate closed before the others got out.

Peter's goat chose that time to start running, too, and it followed Mikkel.

"Whoa!" Peter pulled and tugged on his reins, but it made no difference. The goat had a mind of her own, and she was determined to run or stop without any help from Peter. They bumped over a rock, almost spilling the cart, while Peter still tried to hold the goat back. He looked back for help, but Kurt, Marianne, and Elise were just standing together, laughing again. Peter couldn't help but laugh, too, as he spun out of control around the house. The goat, for some reason, had gotten it into her mind that she would follow the ram, wherever he went. While Mikkel was securing the gate, they were speeding around to the front of the farmhouse, to the gravel courtyard. And there in the middle, out of view from the back, was a shiny black German army staff car, parked by the front door.

Peter tried desperately to stop the cart by pulling back on the reins, but the goat caught sight of the ram, over by the car. Two officers in uniforms were knocking on the front door, with their backs to Peter and the animals. Two younger officers were leaning against the car. When they saw the ram charging them, they jumped up, not knowing what to do.

But the ram knew exactly what to do. He aimed for the two young men, sending them running around to the other side of the large car. The officers at the door, hearing all the yelling, turned around in surprise. By then, Peter was being dragged closer and closer, and he finally decided to bail out by rolling off the cart. He tumbled in the gravel and looked up to see the ram charging the car instead of the men. The big, shaggy animal launched himself horns first into his shiny reflection on the side door of the car. Peter winced at the awful sound as the ram attacked his mirror image with gusto. He backed up, shook his head, and charged again.

"Shoot the animal!" yelled one of the officers, the one who had been knocking on the front door. He came running around the side of the car, drawing a pistol from his holster. By that time Peter's goat with the cart had trotted up to the car, too, and was getting in the way. Peter was sitting in the gravel, wondering what to do next, when Mikkel came sprinting around the corner. The ram crashed into the car once more with a sickening thud.

"Wait!" shouted Mikkel as the officer aimed his pistol.

In a second, Mikkel had bounded across the courtyard, tack-led the ram, and wrestled him to the ground like a cowboy. The officer held his gun up in the air, while Mikkel struggled with the snorting, protesting animal. But when Mikkel sharply snapped the ram with his fingers right between the eyes, the animal seemed to go limp for a moment. Without another word, Mikkel dragged the ram away by the horns, around the corner of the house, leaving Peter still sitting there in the gravel drive-way.

The officer, furious, walked over to the crumpled door of his car. He was sputtering at the others in rapid-fire German. Peter didn't catch many of the words, but he had a good guess what was being said. He didn't have to sit there long before Uncle Harald came around the corner. Mikkel was trotting along be-hind him, the only one in the family who spoke German well enough to communicate with the furious officer.

Uncle Harald turned to his oldest son as they walked up to the Germans. "Ask them what they want," he ordered.

Mikkel asked, and the officer, still red in the face, screamed at Mikkel for several minutes. Peter thought the man might take off, the way he was flapping his arms. But Mikkel just nodded calmly and quietly passed on the translation to his father. Peter was afraid to move, and the goat had found a weed in the gravel to pull up and eat. She looked unconcerned, but the officer ges-tured at the animal, the door of the car, and finally over at Peter. Peter thought about slipping around the back of the house, but he couldn't make himself get up.

This went on for a good five minutes. Then the officer, by then a little calmer, pointed at the two younger men. They had each pulled out a bicycle from the large trunk of the car and were unloading suitcases.

"He says they're going to stay here on the farm for a few months," Peter heard Mikkel tell Uncle Harald. "While they're working at the radar base on Bluewater Hook."

Uncle Harald put his hand on his forehead. *They can't be serious*, thought Peter. Mikkel continued with the translation.

"He says they're each going to need a bed, warm water for washing, breakfast and dinner each day. And he says he'll forget about the car, but the first dinner the men will expect is a roast goat."

The two Germans looked no older than Mikkel. Both wore corporals' uniforms of dull khaki green and small caps. Their jackets were decorated with braids along the shoulders, embroidered with sinister-looking black German eagles over their right front pockets. Their baggy pants were stuffed into the tops of their shiny black boots, which reached almost to their knees. At a word from the officer, each stepped forward.

"Corporal Johann Schneider," announced one. He looked even more boyish than the other.

"Corporal Wilhelm Perlmutter," said the other, clicking his heels.

The officer in charge continued, and Mikkel passed along the instructions.

"He says, these two fine gentlemen . . ." (Mikkel said that sarcastically) ". . . work at the Buffel radar site on Bluewater Hook, and that they will thankfully only be here evenings and Sundays, and then only until a larger barracks is built. Do we have them stay in the field or what?"

Uncle Harald's jaw worked up and down as he decided how to react. There was a moment of uneasy silence. Then he answered his son.

"Tell the officer that his boys will have a room to themselves, and that you will show them the way. Put them in Kurt's room, Mikkel."

Peter shuddered at the thought of these two young men coming to stay. He wished he hadn't agreed to get into the goat cart. The day that had started out as the most fun of the whole holiday had suddenly turned very gloomy.

CLOSE CALL

That night, the Ringsteds and their new houseguests had mutton for dinner—instead of the ram that had charged the car.

"Dad says the ram is much too valuable to destroy," Marianne whispered to Elise as they prepared the dinner. She checked to see that no one was listening, besides Peter. He was just washing his hands. "This one is a five-year-old ewe who hasn't had any lambs for two seasons. A gummer."

Out in the dining room, the young soldiers sat stiffly at their places, waiting to be served their roast goat. They talked to each other, smoked, and looked nervously around at the walls. No one said anything to them, and when one of the men asked a question in German, the family would answer in Danish. Peter tried to rush through on his way back to his bedroom from the kitchen, but one of them grabbed his arm.

"When's dinner?" asked the man, crew cut and dark haired. He acted out eating with a fork, and then pointed to his watch. Peter pretended he didn't understand, wanting to get away.

"Ich verstehe nicht," said Peter, pulling his arm free. That was one thing he knew how to say well in German. "I don't understand."

The man frowned as Peter escaped down the hall, and Peter closed the door behind him as he slipped into Mikkel's bedroom. Kurt was there already, sitting on the bed.

"Did you get away, too?" Kurt bounced a ball on the floor beside the bed.

"Yeah," answered Peter. "One of them grabbed my arm, though, and wanted to know when dinner was being served. They were just sitting there at the dinner table, waiting."

Kurt bounced his ball higher, trying to hit the ceiling. His mother had always told him to keep the ball outside, but just then, no one wanted to go out in the hall or past the dining room. "We're just going to have to keep those two guys out of the barn, that's all."

"Right, but has anyone told the captain yet?" Peter pulled the shade and looked out the window. The barn was on the other side of the house.

"My brother told him all about it. We decided that we're going to have to keep the door to the cellar closed more, especially in the mornings and evenings, when these German guys are supposed to be off work and hanging around here. And if there's any emergency, we tap three times on the door. He has a gun."

"Really?" Peter hadn't seen one.

"Mikkel got it for him."

———

Over the next few days, the kids tried to get used to their new schedule. Mornings and evenings were extra tense, with the soldier "guests" around. The Germans ate a lot, gesturing for whatever they needed at the breakfast and dinner table. The few Danish words they knew were "More milk. More butter.

More meat." They made themselves understood.

Mikkel and Kurt decided that someone would watch the two Germans at all times, or at least know where they were. "That way," said Kurt, "they can't snoop around the house, or especially around the barn, without us knowing it. And Mikkel said he might be able to learn something from what they're doing."

As it turned out, the two soldiers showed little interest in the farm, only in getting fed on time. They spent much of their free time during the evening listening to records on Aunt Hanne's gramophone player, reading, smoking, and sleeping. But they left every morning at six-thirty sharp, riding their bicycles down the road to their radar base. They came back the same way at six-thirty in the evening. In that way they were predictable, and everyone in the house just avoided them as much as they could.

There were two other changes brought by the visitors, aside from the obvious one of hiding the captain more carefully. For one thing, Peter and Kurt now shared Mikkel's bedroom. Aunt Hanne brought them each a thick winter blanket, which they used as sleeping mats on the floor. Every morning, they rolled up their bedding and stuffed it under Mikkel's bed.

The other big change was that Uncle Harald could no longer listen to the BBC every evening. No one said anything with the soldiers around, but Peter could tell when his uncle started slamming doors around six-thirty in the evening that he was fuming again. After dinner on Thursday, when it was Peter's turn to clear the table, he heard his uncle muttering under his breath something about "stuffing those Germans in the root cellar instead of the captain." Then Uncle Harald stalked out through the living room, where the Germans were sitting in his chairs and filling the room with their foul-smelling blue cigarette smoke. The two men were fighting over parts of a German-language newspaper, throwing the paper around and laughing loudly.

In the kitchen, Elise handed Peter a wet dishrag and whispered in his ear. "I'll be glad when we can at least get the captain out of here. Uncle Harald is going crazy." Peter peeked out into the living room, where the two soldiers were still clowning. They had certainly made themselves at home.

Days after that weren't as bad, when Johann and Wilhelm went to work. That's when Peter, Elise, Kurt, and Marianne visited with Captain Whitbread, in between chores. There was just enough room for the two boys to squeeze down the ladder. Elise and Marianne would usually lie on the barn's wooden floor and hang their heads over the edge of the hole, trying to get into the conversation. The captain seemed to enjoy the company, even though Peter could tell he was still hurting a lot—especially his head. The bruises on the man's face were healing slowly, though, and he smiled when they came to visit. Friday afternoon, he looked up when he heard the sound of Elise's voice.

"Ready for another Danish lesson?" she asked him. Over the past several days, that had become their favorite way to start a conversation. He was even learning a few basic words; Elise was a good teacher.

"Ja," replied the captain, sitting up on his elbow. "Goddag." The captain had at least mastered the Danish words for "yes" and "hello."

"Goddag, kaptajn," said Peter, climbing down the ladder. It was musty and a little damp down in the root cellar, but no one seemed to mind. The captain, especially, was very good-humored about all the time he had to spend hiding down there. Peter wished the man's head injury would get better sooner, though, so they could all climb out of there. But then he almost forgot—there were the German guests to deal with. Besides, it was raining hard that morning, and there was nowhere else to go.

Elise handed down a plate, covered with a checkered napkin. "Lidt brød?" she asked.

Peter took the plate and passed it on to the captain. He repeated Elise's question. "Lidt brød?"

The man seemed to understand when he saw the small loaf
of bread under the napkin. "Oh, bread. Some bread?"

Peter and Elise both smiled, just as Kurt and Marianne came
into the barn. "You're just in time for another Danish lesson,"
she reported to them. The cousins bent over and looked down
into the cellar with her.

"Okay, your turn, captain," Elise called down from above in
English. "May I please have some bread, in Danish, is 'Maa jeg
gerne have lidt brød.' "

The captain slowly repeated after her until he got to the last
word. Then he paused, trying to form his mouth around the
strange sound. "Brud? Was that the word for bread?"

Peter laughed. "Brød. Brød." The Danish "ø" sound in the
middle of the word came from deep in Peter's throat, and it
sounded nothing like the captain's proper English. The "d"
sound was swallowed, too, in a way only the kids could understand. But Peter didn't know how to explain all that. They
laughed again as Captain Whitbread tried to mimic him.

"Brode? Brud?" The man shook his head and leaned back on
his pillow. He had raised his head too fast, and he frowned in
pain again. "That's as close as I can get, I'm afraid. Actually, the
way you say it makes it sound rather, well, unappetizing." He
took a big bite of Aunt Hanne's fresh bread. "Mmm. Quite good,
actually. You must thank your mother for the excellent snack.
Especially under these circumstances."

Peter was about to continue the Danish lesson when he heard
the barn door fly open, and Mikkel's voice above them came in
an urgent whisper.

"Everybody out! Close the door up. There are Nazis coming
down the driveway again, fast!" No one said anything; Peter
flew up the short ladder as if he had wings. Then he helped Kurt
lower the door into place, and they kicked hay all over the floor.

They knew what they were supposed to do, but this was not supposed to happen.

"Come on," Mikkel ordered. "We have to look like typical farm kids doing their work." He turned for the door, but a German soldier blocked the way. Had he seen what they were doing?

"Excuse me," Mikkel turned to the soldier. "Can I help you?"

The soldier only grunted and motioned with his rifle for the four of them to stand aside. Behind him was another soldier, who was also tight-lipped and grim. Peter gasped to himself when he saw him. *The man in the back of the church! The one who left when Pastor Kai was preaching against the German invaders!* Only then, he hadn't been wearing his uniform. Peter tried not to stare as they started poking their rifles into piles of hay, looking behind equipment, checking into stalls. He couldn't help starting to sweat, and for a minute, he felt as if he might faint. Elise caught his eye and shook her head, her signal for "Don't stare." One of them, the first one to come in, stood directly on the trapdoor hiding the pilot.

The second soldier, the one Peter had seen before in the church, went from stall to stall in the old barn, while Peter, Elise, and the Ringsteds stood as still as statues. When the soldier got close to the trapdoor he stopped, as though trying to pick something out of the air. Peter thought he could detect the faint smell of the fresh bread. The soldier stared straight at him, and Peter looked to the side. Then the door flew open again, and Uncle Harald marched in.

"Dad!" cried Kurt, his voice cracking. "I'm glad you're here. They're looking for something, but nobody will—"

Kurt stopped in midsentence when he saw the rifle pointed at his father's back. Another soldier marched in behind Peter's uncle, and Kurt drew back.

"Dad?" Kurt choked. Marianne squeezed her eyes shut and held Elise's hand.

"Just do as they say, kids." Uncle Harald squeezed out the words. His face was tight and serious. No one dared look at the floor, or even at the soldier who was still standing right on top of the trapdoor.

The soldiers scraped through the barn for a few more minutes, until an officer finally came striding in. This was not the same one that had brought the two soldiers last Tuesday. He glanced at the floor, then lifted his feet and checked the bottom of his boots, as if not wanting to step in anything. Then he walked over to Uncle Harald.

"Now, Herr Ringsted," began the middle-aged man. His hair was graying, and he wore his officer's cap high on the top of his head. "If you will just show us now where this spy is hiding, you can have dinner with your family, and we can all go home. We have reason to believe—" He waved his hand around the barn. "We have reason to believe with *certainty* that you know something of this man."

Peter noticed that this man's Danish was better than most. That made it easier to listen to, but no less scary, especially with all the guns being pointed. He tried to think if they had let anything slip, if there was any way the two men staying with them could have learned anything about Captain Whitbread. There was only the faint smell of the bread, but Peter thought maybe he was imagining that. If the Germans had found out, wouldn't they have just come in and opened up the trapdoor?

"I would like to put away these guns and not be so dramatic, ja?" continued the officer. He managed a smile and seemed almost pleasant. Too pleasant.

Uncle Harald's expression didn't change, and he looked around the barn. "I would like that, too," he said, his voice flat. "But I cannot tell you about this man, whoever he is, and wherever he is. I simply do not know."

At that, the officer's expression changed to snarling watchdog with a snap of his fingers.

"You don't know?" hissed the man. He spit down at the hay, and Peter was almost surprised that flames didn't shoot up from the spot. "Our dogs found the hiding place out in your fields. Perhaps a short visit with our interrogation team will help clear your head. You should save yourself the trouble, Herr Ringsted. Remember, you are a family man, no?"

With a wave of his hand, the officer dismissed his men, and they herded Uncle Harald out the door in front of their rifles. Peter saw Mikkel tighten up, as if he would spring out at the soldiers like a cat, but then the older boy thought better of it. So they stood there until Uncle Harald was gone, until he had left with a roar in the German staff car. Aunt Hanne came running out the front door, sobbing.

"Harald!" she cried, looking down the lane at the cloud of dust and smoke behind the last army truck. Marianne ran to her mother, and they stood in the front driveway, crying and holding on to each other. Elise ran over, too, and latched on to them. Peter and Kurt stood in the doorway of the barn, Peter not knowing what to say and Kurt too stunned to say anything. Mikkel hovered there for a moment, then muttered something to himself about Johann and Wilhelm and disappeared back into the barn. Peter heard the trapdoor squeaking open.

In a moment, Mikkel reappeared with Captain Whitbread leaning on his arm. Everyone looked over at them, and Captain Whitbread took a deep breath before he spoke.

"Mikkel has told me what has happened," the pilot said to Aunt Hanne. He spoke slowly and deliberately so that she would better understand. Peter could tell he was leaning heavily on Mikkel's arm. "I also gathered what was taking place from the sounds above my head in the barn." He took another deep breath and winced with pain. Even after the days he had spent in the cellar, resting, he looked pale and pained. "I shall not be a cause of this any longer, and I apologize it has taken so long for me to leave you. Mikkel has been in contact with British forces, and we should be able to learn soon when I will be picked up. I—"

Even though Mikkel was holding him up, the man slumped and almost fell to the ground. Aunt Hanne ran over to them, wiping her tears as she ran.

"Captain!" she scolded. "You are our guest, and you are not well. You must lie down again. I don't know what you are doing climbing up here like this, or why Mikkel let you." She helped Mikkel lead him back into the barn.

"Sorry, Mother," Mikkel apologized as they half dragged Captain Whitbread back to the hiding place. "He made me help him."

"It's not your fault," said his mother, giving up her brief fight. She let Peter take the captain's arm, and she slumped down on the floor just inside the barn door. Marianne and Elise crouched down by her, and Marianne put her arm around her mother. They both started to cry once more.

While Mikkel and Peter helped the pilot struggle down the ladder, Kurt followed along behind in frustration and looked down into the cellar.

"If only those two wouldn't have come here," grumbled Kurt. "Johann and what's-his-name. I'll bet they reported that something was going on here."

"We don't know that," said Mikkel, without looking up. "Maybe they did, maybe they didn't. It really doesn't matter. I just have to find a way to get Dad back and Captain Whitbread out of here as soon as we can." Mikkel helped the man lie back down on his cot.

"Can't we help, Mikkel?" Kurt was still hopeful. "I'll bet Peter has some ideas. He's done this sort of thing before."

But Peter didn't have any ideas; he just wanted to crumple up against the wall, like his aunt. Kurt and his ideas were more than he could take. He knew his cousin meant well, but Uncle Harald had just been taken away, and at the point of a gun! As they climbed back up the ladder into the barn, Kurt pulled him aside.

"What do you think, Peter?"

Peter felt panicky, sweaty, almost as if the soldiers had never left. He shrugged away from his cousin's hand on his shoulder. "Think about what?" He raised his voice and headed for the door. "I think I can't listen to your stupid plan!"

As soon as the words were out of his mouth, Peter wished he could take them back. He stopped and turned around. Kurt was standing like a statue in the middle of the barn, looking as if someone had slapped him in the face.

Why didn't I keep my big mouth shut? Peter asked himself. Of course, he wished Kurt hadn't brought up the subject, either, but he hadn't wanted to hurt his cousin's feelings. Aunt Hanne and the girls, who were still sitting in the barn, stared at Peter. What could he do?

"Look. I-I'm sorry, Kurt," Peter stammered. "It's just that . . . well, it's hard to explain."

Peter thought back to last year, when he had helped his Jewish friend Henrik escape to Sweden. At the time, it seemed like the only thing he could do. But now, having the German soldiers searching the barn, it made him shake all over again. He put his hand to his forehead.

This is too much like rowing Henrik to Sweden, he thought. When the German officer was asking Uncle Harald questions in the barn about the hiding pilot, Peter had remembered another German officer, back home, asking his other uncle where the Jews were. *Now it's the same. Only instead of Jews, the Germans are looking for Englanders. They're always looking for somebody.*

Everything was too much like a bad nightmare coming back again and again. Over and over. Peter couldn't even imagine thinking about a plan, or escaping, one more time. He just wanted to be a kid, away from this war. But how could he explain all that to his cousins when he wasn't even sure about it himself?

"Peter?" Elise stood up and came over to him. "Are you all right?"

Peter didn't look up, just nodded his head. "I'm okay," he whispered. But he wasn't okay. Not at all. Elise held on to his shoulders as if he would teeter and fall, which was still possible, the way Peter felt.

"You don't act like it," said Elise firmly. "What's with you?"

"Listen," Peter finally answered, standing on his own. "It's just that I remember what happened to us last year in Helsingor, okay?" Then he turned to Kurt. "I don't know how else to explain this. My best friend Henrik, who was Jewish—I mean he *is* Jewish—we had to hide him in our apartment with a bunch of other Jewish people that the Germans wanted to capture. Then we had to get them over to Sweden, but we ended up . . ." He looked over at his sister. "Elise and I rowed him across the Sound to Sweden by ourselves. It was scary. I don't know, maybe it doesn't bother her. But now it's like . . . it's like it's happening all over again, and I just don't want to think about it anymore. There's nothing we can do about it anyway."

That was all he could say. If he talked anymore, Peter knew he would start crying, or do something embarrassing, and he hadn't cried for years—at least not in front of anybody. Kurt took a step toward the door.

"Sorry, Peter," murmured Kurt. "I didn't mean to . . . I don't know. . . . I thought we could help, or do something to help Pastor Kai and my dad. Maybe the captain, too. You know what I mean?"

"Well, whatever your new plan is, Kurt," interrupted Mikkel, "you can all just forget about it." Aunt Hanne nodded in agreement. "Especially you, Kurt. You have no idea what you're talking about."

"I do too know what I'm talking about!" He turned to face his big brother, ready for a fight. Kurt could switch from sorry to combat in a matter of seconds.

"Don't get mad at him, Mikkel," Peter jumped in. "It's not his fault. It's just me. It's just me, that's all."

"No, it's not just you, Peter," disagreed Mikkel. "Kurt here just has a little growing up to do."

"Growing up?" replied Kurt. "Just because you're nineteen, doesn't mean—"

"Boys!" Aunt Hanne stood up and waded into the face-off between her sons. She may have been small, but she didn't hesitate to act as referee when she needed to.

Mikkel turned to his brother. "Listen, Kurt, I'm not trying to be mean to you or anything like that. But whatever your plan was, you just can't go out and play war. We need to get Dad home somehow, and Captain Whitbread needs to get back to England, but it isn't a game. You've got to get that into your little head." He shook his head as he said it.

"But we can still—" Kurt wouldn't give up. He was interrupted by a muffled voice from the cellar. Everyone had forgotten about Captain Whitbread, who had probably heard them arguing. They walked over to the cellar door and looked down at the man on the cot. Peter thought it was an odd way to talk to someone, almost as if he were down in a grave. Captain Whitbread leaned up on his elbow.

"Excuse me," he began, clearing his throat. "I couldn't help overhearing you, and even though I cannot understand what you were saying, I know I am the cause of your troubles." He was talking slowly, deliberately, even slowly enough for Peter to catch nearly every word. But he was not smiling, and Peter could tell the man was dead serious. Everyone nodded. "As I tried to say already, you've all done quite enough. Today is Thursday, and we should hear any time when I am to be picked up. And you children—no more trying to help. It is simply too dangerous. I am quite serious about this. Do you understand?"

Peter looked down at the floor and traced a circle in the straw with his foot. Everyone else was quiet, even Kurt. They understood.

"Kurt," said Peter quietly, "Captain Whitbread is right. There's nothing we can do."

Kurt still didn't say anything, and Marianne stuck close to her mother. No one replied. After all this, Peter just wanted to get away by himself for a while, to sort things out in his head. "I'm going to go for a little walk," he said to no one in particular. "Just out to the fields."

Before anyone could object, Peter backed out as fast as he could, hoping to escape the feeling of slow, steady panic that still gripped him. Everything about Uncle Harald being taken away and about hiding the captain made him tremble inside.

Despite the heavy rain, Peter pushed through the dripping woods in back of the farm, heading in the direction of the bay, hoping to escape the feeling. Then he cut sideways to a fenced field full of sheep.

Once out of the woods, a flash of lightning made Peter jump. A crack of thunder followed in a few seconds. The storm seemed to be blowing in from the ocean. He stood still, letting the rain fall over him, feeling it turn to hail, then back to rain. He watched a group of sheep grazing behind their fence. Their bodies steamed in the rain, while he was wet and cold. They stared at him, chewing their grass with their big circle chews. Then Peter heard someone call his name.

"Hey, Peter!" called Elise. "Wait up!" Peter thought for a moment of hiding, but he wasn't mad at his sister. He wasn't mad at anyone, really, and he still felt bad for the way he had yelled at Kurt.

"Over here," he called, and Elise came trotting up to where he was leaning on a fence post.

"What are you doing out here?" asked Elise, catching her breath.

"Just looking at the sheep. Thinking."

"In the rain?" They stood there for a few minutes, watching the sheep, listening to the rain on the leaves around them.

Finally Elise spoke up again. "I just wanted to tell you I was sorry," she said, standing awkwardly in front of him.

"Sorry for what? Nothing's your fault."

"Maybe. But I think I've been feeling the same things as you, only I just never say anything."

"Really?" Even though they were twins, sometimes it seemed to Peter that they lived in two different worlds. He was just never sure of what his sister was thinking.

"Yeah." Elise's soft voice was almost lost in the downpour. "I mean . . . well, maybe not exactly the same. I wasn't right there all the time last year with all the things that happened to Henrik." She put her hand on his shoulder. "But I get scared, too."

Even though he was soaked by now, Peter was starting to feel a little better again, for the first time in days. This was the longest conversation he and his twin sister had had in a long time. He felt a little smile on his face, and it was too late to pull it back.

"Thanks," he said, wondering if he needed to say anything else.

"One thing, though, you were wrong about." Elise sounded more like Big Sister Elise again.

"Besides yelling at Kurt, you mean?"

"Well, yeah, but I wasn't thinking about that. It was when you said we can't do anything about what happens." She looked straight at Peter and wiped the wet hair out of her face. "But we can, see? Remember when we prayed at the pastor's house? I think God showed us the radio."

Peter wasn't used to hearing this kind of thing from his sister. But he remembered, and he nodded. He had a pretty good idea that she was right, as usual.

"I remember, Elise. You really think God did that?"

"I wasn't sure then, but I've thought about it now, and I really think so. It happened because the pastor's little boy made us pray."

"I don't know." Peter wanted to believe that, but he still wasn't sure. "Don't you think it would have happened anyway?"

"I just told you what I thought. All I can say is that when we pray, things happen. Like on the boat, going over to Sweden, how everything happened? I was praying."

"You, too? I thought it was just me."

Elise laughed, and it broke the tension. "You're not the only one in this family who prays, Peter Andersen." She turned from him, and Peter thought she was going to run back toward the house. Then she stopped short and turned around.

"But Peter, I wish—" Her hair was all pasted down on her forehead, and she looked almost funny. Peter could tell she wanted to say something important.

"You wish what?"

"I wish . . . well, I'm glad you're praying. That's great. But there's more, like—" For the first time that he could remember, his sister was struggling for words. She started again. "Look, Peter, I may not be the best one to tell you this, but I just wish you would accept Jesus."

Peter gulped. That wasn't quite what he had expected. The year before, his Uncle Morten had told him the same thing. Peter had put it off then. Now everybody seemed to be talking about it—his sister, his aunt, Pastor Kai. . . .

"Accept Jesus?" he asked. "Just like that?" He was stalling for time, time to think. But his sister just stood there in the late afternoon rain, looking at him with her hands on her hips, waiting for him to say something else.

"No," she answered finally. "Not just like that. You've been thinking about it, haven't you?"

Peter wondered what he should admit to. "A little, I guess. But what about you?" That was another stall.

"I already told you about that, in the barn with Jakob." She shifted her weight from her left to her right leg. "I was just a little girl. But it's not hard, you know."

Peter couldn't think of any more ways to avoid his sister. Elise stepped back to where Peter was standing and looked straight at him.

"I'll pray with you if you want." She made it sound like a question. But by that time, Peter knew the answer, and he nodded. With only the sheep as an audience, the two of them bowed their heads in the pouring rain, and Peter finally stopped running from God.

"I'm sorry, God," he began, and from there his prayer tumbled out. Tears mixed with rain, and Elise started to cry, too. When he finished, he looked up at her, and she was smiling. He felt like smiling, too, and the panicky feeling in his stomach— the one that had followed him for the past week—was gone for the first time.

They stood together quietly, peering through the rain, not knowing what to say. A sheep bleated in the distance. Elise smiled and began to sing a familiar children's song: "Baa, says the little lamb; Mama, I'm frozen, want to go home. . . ."

Peter started to laugh when a sudden flash of movement out of the trees caught his eye. He looked at the sheep again.

"Look!" He grabbed his sister's wrist. "What's that?"

They both turned to see a large, dark dog flash through the meadow and head straight for the sheep. The German shepherd barked furiously, and instantly the sheep scattered. Peter didn't know where the dog came from, but it looked as if it would easily hunt down any animal it wanted. Without a thought, Peter jumped over the fence on his side of the small field and sprinted straight for the dog.

"Hey! Yah!" he yelled at the top of his lungs. "Get out of here! Yah!" He clapped his hands as he ran at the dog. By then one of the sheep had fallen, and the dog had a mouthful of wool and had its paws on top of the sheep, trying to keep it down. Peter didn't know what he would do when he got to the wolflike animal, but he knew he wasn't going to let it tear this sheep apart. It looked like a yearling, a lamb that had been born that spring.

He was within four or five steps of the struggling lamb and the snapping dog when he heard a deep, low rumble from the dog's throat. Peter stopped, and the dog looked up without loosening its grip on the petrified sheep. There was fire in the German shepherd's eyes, and it made Peter shiver. He realized then it wasn't the kind of animal he could just clap at and it would shy away.

A stick! I need something to club this monster. Lord, help! He looked around at the ground, but all he could see were a couple of baseball-sized rocks. They would have to do.

Getting still closer, he picked up a rock and took aim, then threw as hard as he could. He hit the dog on the side, but it hardly flinched. *What is this, a wolf? Where did it come from?* The petrified lamb was on its back by then, making an awful sound and pedaling its legs in fear and helplessness. All the other sheep had retreated to the opposite end of the field. The dog still wouldn't let go and growled even louder. Peter picked up the second rock and was getting ready to throw it when he heard a loud whistle, off to the side.

The dog responded instantly, letting go of the lamb and trotting casually back to where its owner, a German soldier, was leaning against a fence post. The man, young and steely eyed, stepped on the barbed wire to open up a large hole for the dog to hop back through. Then the soldier clipped a leash onto its collar and patted its back.

"Gute Hund," he praised the dog, loud enough for Peter to hear. "Good dog."

The soldier chuckled, turned away with the dog, and melted back into the woods. Peter just stood there in the rain, staring. *So this is how the other sheep were killed,* he thought, tightening his fists, *the day they found Captain Whitbread.* Peter knelt down and helped the lamb roll over onto its feet. At least this lamb looked okay, as far as Peter could tell. Terrified, it ran straight back to its mother.

Elise ran up to him. "Are you okay?" she asked, breathless. "I thought you were that dog's next meal, the way he growled at you."

Peter's legs were a little wobbly, but other than that, he felt strangely normal, even good. He wondered about that, considering he had almost entered a wrestling match with an attack dog. "I'm fine." This time he meant it. "You heard it growling all the way over there?" he asked.

"Yeah, but I didn't see that soldier until he whistled."

Peter took a deep breath of relief, then looked over at the sheep. The lamb that had been attacked was back at its mother's side, pulling up tufts of grass, looking as if nothing had happened.

"Peter, don't you think we better go back to the house now?" asked Elise. "We're both totally soaked."

"Yeah, let's go." He looked over his shoulder at the animals and followed his sister back through the woods.

MYSTERIOUS WARNING

Aunt Hanne disappeared from the window before they walked through the front door, but Peter had seen her keeping watch as he and his sister had come into the yard. She met them at the door with two dry towels and a concerned look.

"A little wet out there?" She handed each of them a towel.

"You should have seen it!" said Elise, rubbing her hair dry. Marianne was in the corner of the kitchen, knitting; Kurt was peeling carrots, and Mikkel was fiddling with the family radio. Almost time for the BBC at six-thirty. Peter looked around quickly. For a Friday night, something was different.

"What happened to Johann and Wilhelm?" he asked.

Mikkel looked up from his radio. "Out on the town, I hear. They got a ride back from the radar base, grabbed a couple of things, and left right before you got home. Said they're gone for the weekend. But what happened with you two?"

"There was this dog," explained Elise, "this German shepherd, and it got through the fence at the pasture out past the woods, and—"

"Are the sheep all right?" interrupted Marianne.

"Well, yes, but Peter ran out there and scared it off."

That was only half true, Peter knew. He couldn't let that one pass. "Well, not quite," he explained. "I didn't scare it away, Elise."

She looked at him, as if they had a secret. "From where I was standing," she said, "it sure looked like it."

"You ran in there after the dog?" asked Kurt. He looked impressed.

"I guess I did." Peter shrugged. "But I couldn't get him to let go of the lamb."

Now Mikkel was interested, and he looked up from his radio. "What do you mean, let go? The dog got hold of a lamb?"

"Yeah," said Peter quickly. "But it's okay, I'm pretty sure. Just a mouthful of wool. The dog didn't do anything when I threw rocks at it, only sat there and growled, until the soldier whistled."

Now Aunt Hanne jumped into the conversation. "You say there was a soldier out there? You better explain the whole thing now." She sat them all down at the kitchen table, and it took Peter and Elise several more minutes to explain the whole story, minus the part where they prayed. Peter wasn't sure if he wanted to share that part, not yet.

Aunt Hanne just sat there, taking it all in. When they were done, she sighed deeply and shook her head. "I'm so sorry you two have had to go through all this." She reached over and touched Elise's hand.

"It's all right, Aunt Hanne," said Elise.

"Yeah, really, Aunt Hanne," echoed Peter. "It's all right. If we hadn't been there, the dog would probably have chewed the poor sheep up."

"That's not the point, my dear nephew." Aunt Hanne was warming up for a speech. "The point is that I promised my sister we would take good care of you two, and that you would be out of harm's way here. But as soon as you arrive, the entire German army, not to mention the British Royal Air Force, comes and lands in our living room." She waved a hand toward the barn, where Captain Whitbread was probably settled down for the evening. "And now your Uncle Harald is gone."

For a minute, she looked as if she couldn't say anything else. Marianne scooted her chair over and put her arm around her mother's shoulder.

Then Aunt Hanne took a deep breath, and her lower lip trembled. "As much as I hate to say this," her voice quivered, "it would be safest for you both if you returned to Helsingor a little early."

"Mom, what are you saying?" Kurt stopped peeling carrots.

"I'm saying," replied his mother, "that our farm has turned into a battle zone, and it's no longer the safest place in Denmark for your cousins." She put her head down on the tablecloth. "If only Harald were here."

"Hey, everybody, I've got it," called Mikkel from the other side of the room. With his ear to the radio, he hadn't seen or heard how upset his mother was.

"Mikkel, can't we listen to the news program tomorrow?" asked Marianne.

Mikkel didn't move his ear. "No way. They might give us our confirmation tonight. Our message to tell us when they're coming to get the Englander."

Peter had almost forgotten about the radio message they were supposed to hear on the BBC. What was the code name again?

"Listen for the guy to say 'Dagmar' something, okay?" Mikkel turned their radio up as loud as it would go. Still, it hissed and growled like ocean waves during a storm. They could make out a few words floating through the cloud of noise. It was the BBC, all right. Aunt Hanne dabbed at her eye with a cloth napkin and turned her chair around to face the living room.

"And now," came the voice, "a few greetings to our . . ." It drifted out again, and Mikkel pressed his ear to the large speaker until it came back. ". . . on their fiftieth anniversary. And to our friend Dagmar, whose birthday is tonight, friends will gather at ten forty-five for a wonderful fish dinner. Jens also greets Jorgen, who would like to . . ." And the announcer went on to greet a list of others. Mikkel finally flipped the radio off.

"Was that it?" asked Kurt. "What was that birthday stuff all about?"

"Don't you remember what I told you about how the message would come?" Mikkel was the teacher again. "Dagmar was us, I mean, Captain Whitbread. We already know where they will pick him up—fifty-five degrees, thirty-three minutes, thirty seconds." He looked down at the notes he had taken and pulled out a map. "Fifty-five, thirty-three is just down the coast from the lighthouse on the Hook. Closer to us. And the party is tonight at ten forty-five."

"Ten forty-five! Tonight!" Kurt whistled, low. "How are we going to get him out there to the beach, and who's going to pick him up? It's already seven."

"First of all, Kurt, 'we' are not going to get him anywhere, or maybe you've forgotten that already. You are going to stay right here at home, take care of the sheep, and wait for Dad to get back." Mikkel crossed his arms, ready for another fight. "And the captain's going to catch a fish dinner. I mean, a submarine."

"Wow!" said Kurt, still impressed. "Really a submarine?"

"Really, Kurt." Mikkel was growing impatient. "But we won't see it, I mean, I won't see it. I just have to get this guy to the beach, blink a light, and that will be the end of it."

"And speaking of the end of it," said Aunt Hanne, "our dinner has just about cooked away, it's been on the stove so long. Before you run off, Mikkel, would you please try to call the train station in Varde, to find out when the trains are running tomorrow?"

Peter suddenly felt hungry, and he gladly sat down to a bowl of steaming carrot and potato stew. He was glad the two soldiers were gone tonight, otherwise, how would they have been able to listen to the radio? But he was disappointed that he and Elise would have to leave early, and he looked over at his sister. She gave a little shrug with one shoulder that told him she was disappointed, too. But he knew she was too polite to say anything, especially not to Aunt Hanne. Before he had eaten half a bowl, Mikkel came into the kitchen.

Aunt Hanne quizzed him with her look. "Well? How often does the train run?"

"It doesn't," replied Mikkel. "Rail lines have been blown out by some of my friends from Varde, and no trains are going out of here for at least a week."

Aunt Hanne slumped in her seat and sighed. "Are you sure? Who told you that?"

"Mom, I called a contact in the city, and he told me the story. Then I called the railroad, and they said the same thing. They said it would take at least three or four days to fix. Maybe longer. The Nazis are going to be stomping mad."

"But why would anyone want to do that?" asked Kurt, looking up from his stew.

Mikkel frowned. "Think about that for a minute. Why would anyone want to slow the Germans down? People have been blowing up track all over the country for the past year. I'm just surprised it took so long to get *this* track."

"Oh," replied Kurt. Then his face brightened. "Then that means Peter and Elise can still stay for a while longer!"

A hint of a smile crossed his mother's face, but then she caught herself and shook her head. "It looks as if we don't have much choice in the matter, do we?"

Kurt reached over and pumped Peter's hand, as if congratulating him. It made Peter feel a little silly, but he was glad to be able to stay, even for just a few more days.

Aunt Hanne was clearing a bowl from the table when their conversation was interrupted by a sharp knock on the front door. Peter looked at his aunt, and he thought she might drop what was in her hands.

Marianne pushed her chair back and jumped to her feet. "I'll get it!" she called out.

"No!" said Aunt Hanne, putting down her bowl. "Your father wouldn't have knocked. I'll get it."

But Mikkel was already halfway across the room, and he carefully cracked open the door. Mrs. Steffensen, the pastor's wife, stood there in the doorway, trying to catch her breath, looking into the living room. She was half sobbing, half choking, and completely soaked. Little Jakob stood behind her, clinging to her leg. Mikkel swung the door open all the way. Aunt Hanne gasped and rose to her feet.

"Ruth!" she cried, rushing over to her friend. "What are you doing out there in the rain? Is something wrong? Come in!"

Marianne went to get towels for them to dry off with, and Aunt Hanne found them chairs. Mrs. Steffensen couldn't say anything at first, between sobs.

"It's Kai," she finally managed. "A note." Then she burst into tears again and buried her head in her hands. Aunt Hanne kneeled next to the chair and put her arm around the pastor's wife, while Marianne came with towels. Little Jakob didn't say anything, but his eyes were wide with fright.

"What kind of note?" asked Aunt Hanne. "Is there something we can do?"

Mrs. Steffensen, still unable to talk, fished a crumpled envelope out of her coat pocket and handed it to Aunt Hanne.

"Priest . . ." Aunt Hanne began, then paused. She scanned the note quickly while everyone else waited. Then she handed it over to Mikkel. "My German's not so good. Mikkel?"

Mikkel straightened out the wet, crumpled letter. Then he read, pausing to translate the meaning. "Priest." He squinted at the note, trying to make out the letters. "You are on the list of troublemakers to be killed. Hide now. Get . . . away. Do not go to Oksby. Do not tell anyone that you were warned, or I will be . . ." Mikkel fished for the word, ". . . um, punished." He looked up at Mrs. Steffensen, and his face showed the same shock that everyone else must have felt. Peter gripped his chair.

"Where did this note come from?" Aunt Hanne asked her friend.

"Jakob found it on the front porch just a short while ago," explained Mrs. Steffensen, who by then had started to catch her breath. "I looked out, and I saw a young man running away down the path. No one I recognized, not from around here. He couldn't have been more than eighteen or nineteen, I would guess."

"There's a little more of the note," said Mikkel.

"A signature? Who wrote it?" asked Kurt.

"No, not a signature, of course not." Mikkel shook his head quickly. "For sure it wasn't anyone in the Underground. But who else would know, besides a German?" Mikkel turned to the pastor's wife. "He wasn't wearing a uniform, was he?"

Mrs. Steffensen thought for a moment. "I don't think so, no. He had a coat on, not an army coat, but his pants were army gray. Yes, he was wearing army pants!"

"So why would a German write this note?" asked Peter.

"If he *was* a German, I sure don't know," said Mikkel, rubbing his cheek. "But listen to this last part. It says, 'God will not forgive those who kill the priests.' "

"Wow!" Kurt whistled, the way he did when he was impressed. "Guilty conscience or something. You think it really was a Nazi, Mikkel?"

"Maybe," said Mikkel, shaking his head. "If it was, he was right about being punished. If anyone found out about the note, this guy would be in as much trouble as the pastor." Then he thought of something. "But where is Pastor Kai?"

"He got a phone call just before this note came," explained Mrs. Steffensen. "And he left quite suddenly. He said it was someone who needed help, but I don't know where he went."

"I know where." It was the first thing little Jakob had said since he arrived. Everyone looked at the small boy.

"You know where he went?" Mrs. Steffensen pulled her little boy up on her lap and looked straight at him. "Why didn't you tell me before?"

"You didn't ask me." Jakob fidgeted. "He went to Oksby. He told me. I ran after him." The little boy didn't quite understand what he had just said, but it hit Peter. *The warning note said not to go to Oksby! And that's where Pastor Kai is headed right now on his bike!*

By then everyone else understood what was happening, especially Mikkel. He punched his hand with his fist.

"I told him!" His voice went up a notch. "I told him already that he was on a list, but, no, he wouldn't believe me. And now look!"

"Mikkel!" His mother tried to quiet him. "It's too late for that now."

"What kind of list?" Jakob still wanted to know. Peter didn't want to be the one to explain to him.

"Never mind, Jakob." His mother sounded more like she was comforting him after he had skinned his knee. She ran her fingers through his short-cropped hair.

Peter imagined Pastor Kai, riding along the wet road on his bicycle, with someone waiting for him in the bushes. *We can't just stand here and talk about it*, he wished he had the courage to say. Instead, he grabbed his jacket, which was still wet from his walk in the rain. Elise must have had the same thought; she went to the closet and pulled out her gray rain slicker as well.

"What do you two think you're doing?" asked Mikkel, putting his hands on his hips.

Peter looked at his older cousin. He felt more sure of this

than almost anything else he had ever done. There was no question what he had to do.

"We're going to catch up to Pastor Kai, if we can," said Peter, matter-of-factly. He started for the door with Elise.

"You can't," Aunt Hanne said nervously. "I can't let you do that."

With his hand on the doorknob, Peter looked back. "I don't mean to sound disrespectful, Aunt Hanne, but don't we have to try? We just have to!"

There was a silent tug-of-war in the room, as everyone looked to Aunt Hanne. She seemed to sway one way, then the other, and she nervously rubbed the back of her neck. Then she looked over at the pastor's wife.

"If only Harald were here," Aunt Hanne finally whispered. Then she looked over at her oldest son. "Mikkel, can you go with them?"

"I could, Mom, but I think it's better if I run into town and get some kind of car. We can take the captain with us, then everyone can wait for the sub at the same time."

The captain! In all the talk about Pastor Kai and Uncle Harald, no one had mentioned the man who needed to escape the most. Peter thought for a second how he was probably huddled down in the root cellar, not able to help make any of these decisions. Mikkel would talk to him.

But by now Mrs. Steffensen was totally confused. Obviously, she didn't know who the captain was, or anything about a submarine, or even why she would have to wait for one. Mikkel looked over at her, and motioned for her to follow him outside.

"Don't worry, Mrs. Steffensen." Mikkel was in motion again. "I'll explain it to you in the car."

It looked as if Aunt Hanne's decision had been made for her, and Peter opened the front door. The deep green smell of the steady rain came drifting in.

"Wait up, Peter," piped Kurt, pulling on his own coat. "Marianne and I are coming, too! Right, Marianne?" In response, Marianne went to the hall closet for her rain slicker.

"Marianne!" Their mother looked helplessly from one person to the next.

"Mom, we'll stay away from anyone on the road, okay?" asked Marianne. She sounded more sure of herself than usual. "All we're going to do is catch up with the pastor. And there are two roads he could have taken to Oksby, so we have to split up."

Peter imagined his map again, and the triangle of roads between the farm, Ho village, and Oksby, or Bluewater Hook. Marianne was right: The pastor could have taken one of two roads. Either way, Peter, Elise, and their cousins needed no more encouragement. Mikkel's strong words from before—about not getting involved—had been put on ice. They were out of the door and running for their bicycles before anyone could change their mind.

"Whatever car we can get," Mikkel shouted out the door, "we're going to cruise around the long way to Oksby and pick you up, okay? I'll take care of the captain. Just remember, all you need to do is catch up with Pastor Kai. I don't want you to do anything if there's anyone else around. Just get to him before anyone else does."

"Right!" Peter shouted back. He was still scared, but he had forgotten all about the sick feeling, the one he had felt so many times before this summer. Something else—he wasn't sure what—had replaced it.

"So do you think they would really hurt him, like the note said?" asked Kurt as they were pulling their bicycles out of the barn. There wasn't even time to talk to the captain.

No one answered. In a minute, they were all on their bikes, pedaling furiously down the long driveway. The dark gray clouds would shorten this long summer night, so Peter figured they had only about two and a half more hours of light. Maybe three. At least the rain had pulled back to a light drizzle. Peter didn't care; he was still wet from his walk.

"How about if Elise and I go the short way, and you two take the longer way around?" suggested Peter. "We know this way, but you know the roads on the loop a lot better."

"Okay," agreed Marianne.

"Yeah," said Kurt. "That way, we'll catch him whichever way he went."

"But how much of a head start do you think he has?" asked Elise.

Marianne cleared her throat. "Depends on how long he stopped on his errand, whatever it was. If he left forty-five minutes ago and stopped for a half hour, we just have to make up about fifteen minutes. It's seven-thirty, right?"

No one answered. They were at the end of the driveway by then, and all of them turned right for the short ride to Ho. They would separate when they made it to Ho village, where Elise and Peter would go left, straight out to Oksby and Bluewater Hook. Kurt and Marianne would continue through the village, riding until they reached the top of the triangle of roads, and then cut off to the left.

"Meet in Oksby?" asked Peter.

"Yeah," agreed Kurt. "You'll get there first. Wait for us at the inn there, unless you see Germans around. Then go to the church."

Peter looked at his sister, but she was already sprinting down the road on her bike. She looked over her shoulder.

"Come on," she called impatiently. "Let's go."

That was the last thing anyone said, then they all saved their breath for riding. Ignoring the bone-jarring bumps of the rutted country road, Peter pretended he wasn't on a wooden-wheeled old bicycle. Instead, he was in the famous Tour de France bicycle race, and they were crossing the French Alps. Everyone else was behind him and his teammate Elise, except for one rider. This was the man they had to catch. He put his head down and pedaled harder than ever, then pulled up even with his sister. Somehow, she kept up with him. They passed two more farms before it was time for the four of them to split up.

Kurt waved as he and Marianne kept going straight down the road. "We'll see who catches up with him first!" Even now, Kurt was the competitor. Peter shook his head as he and Elise turned down the road to Oksby and Bluewater Hook, with Elise ahead slightly. *Would Pastor Kai be on this road?*

"Watch out for big potholes coming up!" Elise's warning snapped him back to the present, but it was too late. His wooden wheel sank hard into a large hole, and the bike jolted to one side. The next thing Peter knew, he was flying over his handlebars. He landed on his hands and knees and skidded in the gravel, then rolled over with the bike.

"Peter!" Elise left her bike and ran back to where he lay. She helped him sit up, and Peter fought back the tears. If this were just a couple of years ago, he would have been howling. Instead, he gritted his teeth while Elise helped him pick out bits of gravel from his knees.

"We don't have time for this," gasped Peter, wobbling to his feet. He checked out his bike. Somehow, the wheel had stayed in one piece, and everything still worked. It kind of wobbled, though, when he pushed it.

"Well, can you keep going?" asked Elise. Peter nodded. Then she slapped him on the back. "Good thing you weren't wearing long pants, or you would have ripped out the knee, for sure."

Peter smiled at the joke. At least, he thought it was a joke. As it was, his right leg was now bleeding down to his socks, and both knees were throbbing with pain.

"I'm fine." Peter hopped back on his bicycle and started pedaling stiffly down the road. He would just have to ignore the pain, no matter what.

The rain stopped, and Elise set up a pace: sprint thirty pedals, cruise thirty pedals. Sprint count to thirty, cruise count to thirty.

After a while, Peter even started to forget about his knee.

"How are you doing?" Elise looked over at her brother as they matched pedal for pedal.

"Okay. I'm doing okay." He looked up ahead, searching for any sign of the pastor. A bike, a man, anything. The land around them had opened up to gently rolling heather-covered hills, mixed in with small patches of woods. Even though the clouds made it darker, they could still see well over the hills toward the sea, especially when they got to the top of each small rise.

A half-mile went by, then one and two, and still there was no sign of Pastor Kai. For that matter, Peter couldn't make out anyone else on the road. If they kept going in this direction, Peter knew they would soon reach Oksby and the ocean. So they kept pedaling, trying to keep their thirty-thirty pace.

"The pastor has to be around here somewhere, don't you think?" Elise asked as they came to the top of a small hill. Peter could see over two smaller hills, and barely made out the road that snaked through the heather on its way to Oksby. He was about to say something but caught his tongue at what he saw.

On the top of the second hill were two other riders coming toward them, the first people Peter had seen. They were a ways off, though, and Peter couldn't tell if he and Elise had been spotted. At the same time, he caught sight of someone else on a bicycle, halfway between Peter and Elise and the other riders. There was no mistaking the dark jacket and long legs. *Pastor Kai!*

Without a word, brother and sister knew what they had to do. If they could reach the pastor before the other two men, maybe they could warn him, and turn around in time to hide. It wasn't much of a plan, but there was a slight chance that the men hadn't seen them yet. The hills and small dips in the road gave them a little shelter. And besides, thought Peter, it was getting darker. Like a mirror image, he and Elise pedaled faster and faster, until they were sprinting all out.

I can't yell, thought Peter, even while he struggled to keep from shouting to the pastor. *And I can't run away.* The thought had crossed his mind—just for a split second—that he could turn around. Instead, he pedaled even harder, furious at the thought that someone wanted to hurt Pastor Kai and his family. Elise kept her eyes straight ahead, straining to keep up.

They can't do it, they can't do it, Peter repeated to himself, in time with the wheels, over and over, faster than he thought possible. They disappeared into another low spot, so Peter stood up and pedaled to see if he could catch another glimpse of the pastor.

They won't do it, they're not going to do it, he repeated, and he was flying over the gravel road. Elise flew right alongside, not falling behind for a second. Peter never imagined she could cycle so fast. He forgot about breathing, about his aching lungs, about his bleeding knees. Everything hurt, and every breath was like breathing fire, but he just kept pedaling.

Together they launched over the top of the next hill as if they had wings. They nearly crashed into Pastor Kai, who was straddling his bicycle, standing between two men and their bikes.

The older one looked up at Peter and Elise, and Peter knew from the look in his eye that this wasn't a friendly visit.

The man was a bit round, and appeared to be sweating, even in the cool weather. He looked out of place with a stiff gray suit and a hat that fell back on his head. This was no farmer.

"Peter!" Pastor Kai looked up, too, in surprise. "Elise. What brings you this way?"

Peter didn't know what to say.

OCEAN WATCH

What do I do now? Peter thought. Between breaths, all he could force out was a weak, "Oh, hi, Pastor Kai." Elise was breathing even harder.

The pastor smiled at Peter. "Catch your breath," he told them. Then he turned to the other men. "Well, gentlemen, as I mentioned, we'd be happy to have you visit the church. And since you asked, our Sunday services are at eleven."

The younger man, who really didn't look much older than Mikkel, looked as if he were waiting for instructions from the other man. "What do you think, Heinrich?" asked the young man. "The kids, too?"

As soon as the younger man opened his mouth, Peter knew he was Danish.

The older man looked straight at Peter, with a piercing gaze that sent shivers up his spine. Peter caught his breath. *This would be a good time to leave*, thought Peter, and the pastor started to push his bike along, too.

At the same time, the older man turned the wheel of his bike to block the pastor's way. He didn't even look over as he answered the younger man. "Yes, the kids, too. They have arrived at precisely the wrong moment." As Peter had guessed, the man spoke with a heavy German accent.

"Excuse me?" asked the pastor. "Did you need something else?" He was obviously puzzled at the odd comments. Peter had a chilling idea what they were all about, though. Elise started to back her bike away, and the German took hold of her handlebar. A sick smile crept over his face as he reached into his jacket and brought out a long gray German pistol and leveled it at Pastor Kai.

"Yes, we do," said the man, and his voice hardened even more. "I do need something else. I need you to remove yourself from your bicycle and kindly walk over there to the edge of the road." He waved the pistol menacingly as he spoke, and Peter could almost feel the poison in the man's words. Now the shiver in Peter's back turned to solid ice. Pastor Kai stared at the end of the gun, then glanced over at Peter and Elise. But there was nothing he could do.

"If you please," repeated the man. "Or shall we stand here all evening, studying the gun?" Then he looked at Elise, who was stiff with fear. "And you two, the young boy and girl, you will do the same."

"Look here," objected the pastor. "I don't know who you are, or what you want, but certainly these kids—"

"They have already seen more than their young eyes should have seen," finished the German. "Regrettable."

"Heinrich," interrupted the other man. "Couldn't we just let them go? Maybe the pastor is right about that—"

The heavy German let his bicycle fall to the gravel and let go of Elise's bike. With his eyes still on the pastor, he took a step sideways. Then with his free hand he grabbed the front of the younger man's shirt, and pulled him around to where he could see him. "You, too, Hans? Do you know what you're saying? What's gotten into you? Perhaps you want to join these two?"

Peter took a step back. Most of the German soldiers he had seen before seemed more like grown-up bullies. Here, Peter felt close to raw evil, evil that smiled, evil that walked and breathed. He prayed silently, without moving his lips.

Lord, I'm scared. Peter shivered. *Please get us out of here, away from this.* And that was all he had time for. The Dane, Hans, withered away from Heinrich's threat.

"No, no," whimpered Hans. "Of course you're right."

Peter looked at the younger man and felt pity for him. The Danes called these people "Stikkers," and they were hated for the way they helped the Germans. But right now Peter was far from feeling hatred; he was only thinking how to get away from Heinrich. He looked over at Elise, and by the look in her eye, he could tell her mind was working, too.

Heinrich pulled out a handkerchief, wiped his brow, and laughed. Still, he kept his gun leveled at Pastor Kai, who was off his bike.

"That's right," said Heinrich. He chuckled, in a strange sort of way. "Find a comfortable place in the ditch there." He waved his gun, then shoved Pastor Kai face first into the mud by the side of the road.

Something snapped inside Peter, and without thinking about it, he lunged at the German's arm, grabbing desperately at the gun.

The man, caught off guard, bellowed like an animal, and swung Peter around with his arm. Peter hung on, kicking and grabbing for the gun, doing everything he could to push the man off balance. Then Peter felt Elise grab an arm, too, and the three of them struggled for a moment.

But Heinrich was bigger and more powerful than Peter had hoped. Instead of falling, he swung Peter all the way around like a merry-go-round and flipped him into the ditch next to Pastor

Kai. He swung at Elise with his gun, hitting her shoulder. Then he pushed her off balance with his boot, sending her sprawling. She rolled once and lay on her back next to Peter, tears in her eyes. But she said nothing.

The German clutched his gun and wheezed from the effort. Peter, Elise, and the pastor looked up at him from the ditch, and to Peter the man seemed more evil than ever. He waved his gun once more, almost like a toy. Then he caught his breath, straightened his coat, and smiled.

"Put up a fight? Why not?" He laughed, and the sound sickened Peter. Pastor Kai reached over and took Peter's hand. Peter felt for Elise. They lay that way for fifteen minutes—maybe longer—while Heinrich strutted back and forth next to the ditch. All the time he babbled on about the war, Germany's victories, and what he thought was a glorious future for his army. The nightmarish speech reminded Peter of the German dictator, Hitler, and he tried to close his ears. Finally, the other man interrupted.

"Heinrich, that's enough!" It was the Dane this time, and he sounded different. His voice was still quivering, though.

"Quiet, Hans," replied the German. The evil returned to his voice, and the smile left his lips. "I believe you are already in enough trouble as it is."

"Not in as much trouble as you will be if you don't drop that gun," announced Hans. Peter couldn't believe what he was hearing. The big man made a motion to turn around.

"No, Heinrich," warned Hans. "Don't turn around. I have a gun, too, you know."

The big man's face turned red with rage. He worked his jaw up and down, as if deciding what to do. Then they all heard the distinct click of Hans's gun.

"I'm not kidding, Heinrich." Hans was almost yelling. "Do it now. Drop your gun. Now!"

"Don't be a fool, Hans," replied the German. "Your life is

over if you go through with this. But we can forget this ever happened if—"

"Shut up, Heinrich, I mean it. It's the other way around now. This is a priest and two kids. I may be a Stikker, but when it gets down to priests and children, that's too far for me."

There was a crack of gunfire as the younger man shot over Heinrich's shoulder, and that was all the convincing the big man needed. He dropped the gun in the gravel at his feet.

"Now, kick it into the ditch," ordered Hans. Heinrich obeyed.

"You kids. Priest," continued Hans. "Get up and get on your bikes. Get out of here, disappear, and forget this ever happened. Now go!"

Pastor Kai pulled Peter and Elise up out of the mud with him, and they tiptoed past Heinrich. Peter didn't look at the man, but he could feel the daggers, even at five or six feet away. Finally, he glanced up at Hans, and the man was shaking. He even pointed his small gun at them as they picked up their bikes.

"Hurry up, Priest," Hans shouted. "I don't even know why I'm doing this, but you better lose yourself pretty quick!"

Peter, Elise, and the pastor didn't look back, didn't say another word as they started to pedal down the road again toward Oksby and Bluewater Hook. Peter thought they must have looked more than odd, all covered with mud, and he almost wished it would rain again, to wash them off. He shivered to think of what would probably happen back there, and he expected the sound of a gunshot any moment. He thought he heard it once, but he wasn't sure. After they were out of sight of the two men, Pastor Kai broke the silence.

"Elise, your shoulder. Is it all right?"

Elise nodded, but Peter could tell she was hurting. She was crying quietly, and her lip quivered.

"Do you want to stop for a minute?" asked Peter.

But Elise shook her head strongly and started pedaling faster.

"No! It's just a bruise. We have to get farther away!"

Peter understood, and he kept pace. The problem was, in their haste to get away from the German, they were going in the opposite direction of home. *Probably Pastor Kai knows people in Oksby where we can stay*, he told himself.

"You realize what almost happened back there, don't you?" asked the pastor.

Peter nodded, and the pastor asked him another question.

"What I want to know is, why did you come riding down the road just then, when those two men had just stopped me?"

Peter explained about the warning, and how Mrs. Steffensen had come to the house earlier that evening.

"My wife!" said Pastor Kai. "And Jakob—they're both all right?"

"They're fine," answered Peter. He was still shaking, thinking about the men, and he felt as if he could start crying, too, he had been so scared. "They're fine . . . but Mikkel said you would all need to leave, right away. Tonight, even."

The pastor shook his head. "I didn't believe him, but now . . ."

They were getting close to a few farmhouses, closer to the sea and to the town of Oksby. Past the town was the radar base where Johann and Wilhelm worked, but of course those two weren't there now. Good thing. Like Mikkel, Peter was almost certain they had something to do with Uncle Harald being taken away. Peter didn't care to ever see them again.

But he didn't have any more time to worry about it. In the distance, Peter could hear a truck, or a bus. It picked up speed, and then he saw it, heading straight for them. They moved over to the edge of the road, leaving as much room as they could. But the bus didn't pass by. Instead, it screeched to a stop in a cloud of gravel, and a man leaned out the driver's window.

"Get in!" shouted the driver.

Peter recognized the voice. *Mikkel!*

The three exhausted riders wheeled their bikes over, and pushed them up the steps into the bus, while Mikkel helped pull them in. Inside, Mrs. Steffensen jumped up from a seat and embraced her muddy husband. Jakob was at her side, and he latched on to his father as well. Captain Whitbread sat in the front seat, propped up with a pillow.

"Okay, people," said Mikkel. "Sit tight. This has got to be the craziest bus ride you will ever take, but we're not there yet."

Peter and Elise sat down behind Captain Whitbread, while Mikkel struggled with the large gearshift. It made a terrible grinding sound, and Mikkel muttered nervously. "Come on, where are you, gears? That's it." Finally they lurched down the road, found a place to turn around, and headed straight back toward Oksby. Peter could smell the salt air blowing in through a crack in the front window. They had to be almost by the beach.

Before they got to town, though, Mikkel quickly pulled off the road and followed a rutted, sandy trail for what seemed like several miles. Ruts and large holes in the trail forced Mikkel to slow to almost walking speed, and the bus lurched like a carnival ride. Peter and Elise both leaned over to try to keep the captain steady. After about thirty minutes of bouncing, Mikkel pulled the bus to a stop, shut off the engine and yanked the brake lever. Then he turned around and spoke in a quiet, determined voice.

"Okay, listen, everybody. We're on Skalling Beach, and there's a little cabin we're going to wait in. We still have a few minutes, so everyone can just get into the cabin and be real quiet. No lights. There aren't any mines on this section of beach, but there are regular patrols. On the hour. Now, go—I have to park this thing, and I'll be right back."

The first one out was the captain, and Elise helped him down the steps. He was too heavy for her, though, and they almost tumbled. Pastor Kai rushed forward, holding on to the man's shoulder from the other side.

"You need some help here," said Pastor Kai, pulling Captain

Whitbread's arm over his own shoulder. "Here, Elise, you take his right side." The two of them helped the struggling pilot down the narrow steps of the bus and out into the night air. As everyone else filed out, Mikkel caught Peter's arm.

"Are you okay, Peter? You look like you've been rolling in the mud. And your leg—" He pointed at Peter's knee.

Peter took a deep breath. He had almost forgotten about the knee, and besides, there wasn't time to explain just then. "It's a long story. We're okay now. I think."

Elise trotted back from behind the small cabin, which was almost hidden next to a sand dune. She seemed to have forgotten about her shoulder, and she looked up at Mikkel, who was still in the seat of the bus. "Are you two coming?"

"Not me," replied Mikkel. He hesitated slightly. "Look, I'm embarrassed to say this, but I—I'm going to need your help again. Believe me, I did everything I could to keep you out of this mess, but it didn't quite work out the way I planned. When the pastor's wife came, and they needed to leave, too, it threw everything off."

Peter nodded. "You don't do all this Resistance stuff by yourself, do you?"

"Well, I wasn't supposed to," replied Mikkel. "There was going to be another guy helping me, but . . . that's where I need your help again." He pulled out a long black flashlight from under his seat, bent down, and glanced briefly at his wristwatch. "Okay, we still have about ten minutes until the German patrol comes by. Every hour, remember. So I have to get this thing out of here right now. But the rendezvous time is supposed to be in fifty-five minutes. Ten forty-five."

Peter wondered how his cousin knew the exact times of all the Germans' comings and goings, but he didn't dare ask. Mikkel twirled the flashlight nervously in his hands and continued explaining.

"Listen carefully now. I'm going to drive the bus back down

the road to the edge of town and leave it there. Someone will see it. I'll try my best to get back right away, but I'm not sure it will be in time for the boat."

"Boat?" asked Peter.

Mikkel nodded. "Rubber raft. You know, from the submarine. They're going to send a rubber raft to pick up the captain. The only thing they don't know yet is that they have three more passengers."

Elise shifted on one foot and leaned against the bus door. "So what do we have to do?"

"Nothing, I hope," replied her cousin. Mikkel ran his hands through his slicked-back hair and looked toward the cabin. "I must be nuts. Captain Whitbread should be doing this, but he's kind of, you know, in and out. You know some Morse code, right, Peter?"

"Yeah," admitted Peter. "I know it, but I'm kind of slow."

Elise spoke up. "He knows the whole thing, backwards and forwards. Last summer, he used to send messages to his friend Henrik down the street all the time with his flashlight."

"Okay, but it probably won't matter," said Mikkel. "Like I said, I'll be back in just a few minutes. But if they're early—" He passed the flashlight over to Peter. "You'll need this."

Peter took the flashlight and moved the switch on and off to test it. The light hit Mikkel in the eyes.

"It works, it works." Mikkel pointed his finger at his cousin. "Listen. Don't use it unless you see a light flashing from out there." He waved in the direction of the ocean. "They'll flash three times—a long flash, another long flash, and then a short flash—for 'D.' You know, Dagmar, our contact name?"

Peter and Elise both nodded.

"Then," continued Mikkel, "we flash back a 'C' for 'Come, all safe,' or an 'N' for 'No, get out of here.' "

"Okay." Peter repeated after Mikkel: "Long-short-long-short for a 'C,' or just long-short for 'N.' "

Mikkel patted Peter's arm. "You know the code. Good. Now, the sooner I get out of here, the sooner I'll be back. Take the light, and keep an eye out. Everyone else knows they're supposed to stay in the summer house. Just leave me one of the bikes."

Peter and Elise rolled their bicycles out to the gravel driveway of the summer house, while Mikkel pulled the bus around and disappeared down the road to town. They hid their bikes in the low bushes next to the little house. Even though the sun had set, Peter could still make out the shape of the place. It was a typical small summer cottage, one of many nestled in the heather-covered dunes, just away from the beach. Only now, it was boarded up because of the war. There was a small light coming from behind the window shutters, a hint that everyone was in there. Elise quietly pushed in the front door, and as Peter followed he felt for a way to lock it behind him.

"There's a latch on the door there," whispered Pastor Kai. He was holding a small candle up to his face. Next to him, his wife and little Jakob huddled in the light. Captain Whitbread rested on a small couch. Everything smelled as if it hadn't been aired out in years.

"I apologize for not being much help to you young people," said the captain. "This was supposed to have been my party, but it's all I can do to keep my head up."

"Don't worry, Captain," said Pastor Kai in English. After what they had been through in the ditch, Peter thought it strange to hear the pastor telling someone else not to worry. "I can imagine this has not been a very cheery experience for you."

"No, hardly," replied the captain. "But you people have made it almost pleasant, in a way, and I thank you for that."

Elise peeked out the window, then turned back to the rest of them. "Mikkel said we're supposed to keep watch out the window in case the submarine comes early. He had to go get rid of the bus." She looked around the small room, which was bare except for a simple picnic table, two old white wooden folding chairs, and a small, weathered couch where Captain Whitbread was lying. In the corner was a sink and a rusty camp stove. Everything else had been stripped from the place, and it looked as if vacationers hadn't used it in years. She looked over at the pastor, who was still holding his candle. "Mikkel also said a German patrol comes by this place every hour. I think we better blow out the candle, don't you?"

"Oh." Pastor Kai lowered his voice to a whisper and quickly blew out his light. "Of course."

As his eyes got used to the darkness Peter thought he saw a large gap in the front window shutters, large enough to look through and see the beach beyond.

"Look here, Elise," he whispered. "We can see everything through this crack." He pulled her head down to see. "If anybody starts blinking out there, I'll just step out the door and blink back."

"Just make sure, young man," instructed Pastor Kai, "that we don't run into any more of our 'friends' with the guns."

Elise found a place on the floor and settled down without saying anything more. Peter was glad when Pastor Kai started talking about something entirely different.

"Elise, did you ever come up with an ending to our poem? I still would like to use it in a sermon sometime, perhaps in a book."

Elise was looking intently out through the window from her spot on the floor. But she straightened out, and in the dim light Peter thought he saw her smile.

"Well, yes," she whispered back. "I think I have some ideas. But is this a good time to tell you?"

"I hate to say this," sighed Mrs. Steffensen, who was sitting next to her husband with her arm around him. "But it may be your last chance for a long while." She seemed nervous, but not as upset as she had been before. Peter guessed she was relieved at least to be with her husband. Little Jakob curled up next to her, holding on to her leg and not saying a word.

"Okay." Elise rested her head against the wall in the darkness. "I remember the part you were working on, so tell me what you think of this: 'I waited patiently through the spring, knowing it couldn't live long. When a frozen blue flower, this delicate thing . . .' That's the part you've already written. Okay, 'When a frozen blue flower, this delicate thing, Brought in its blossom a note from Heaven's song.'"

"Neat," chirped Jakob. It was the first thing he had said all evening. His wide, frightened eyes softened a little, and Elise laughed quietly.

"A note from Heaven's song." Pastor Kai repeated the last line Elise had made up. "I like it a lot. It fits the poem perfectly. Thank you, Elise. I'll remember that."

Peter listened to his sister and the pastor talking and smiled to himself. Here they were, waiting for a submarine in the darkness, with German soldiers probably walking by outside, and they were reciting poetry! It fit right in, though, their poem about hope. Right now, they needed all the hope they could get.

Peter glanced over in the dark room to where he knew the captain was slumped on the couch. He slid over and bent his head closer to hear how the man was breathing.

"How are you doing, Captain?" Peter whispered. He could barely tell that Whitbread nodded without opening his eyes.

Peter could almost feel the man's headache, and he wished there was something else he could do for him. Instead, he glanced out through the crack in the window again and tried to focus his eyes. The best thing he could do for Captain Whitbread—for everyone—would be to see the signal from the submarine. *Look for the "D" signal, then flash back a "C" or an "N."* He practiced the scene over and over in his mind, as if memorizing the lines of a play. *Look for the "D," and then—*

A small flash of light? He wasn't sure. It wasn't time yet. But maybe—

"Elise, look!" He tugged at her sleeve. "I think I saw something!"

Elise leaned over to where Peter had stationed himself, looked over his shoulder and out through the window.

"I don't see anything," she said. "It's still a little early. Mikkel's not back yet. And besides, the Germans are supposed to go by any time now."

"Yeah, but I'm pretty sure I saw something." They waited for a moment more. Then it was there again—a faint but sure light, almost straight out from the beach house, far out on the water.

"Long flash, long flash, short flash," said Elise. Her grip on her brother's shoulder tightened. "It's them! But they're a half hour early."

Captain Whitbread straightened up and tried to stand, but he only rocked around and nearly tipped over. Pastor Kai jumped to his side and tried to hold him straight.

"I've got you, Captain," said the pastor. "We're almost there."

"Thank you," replied Captain Whitbread, trying to find his balance. He twisted his face in pain. "I'll be fine as soon as we get off this beach."

Peter got to his feet and tried to sound confident. "Okay, I'll go outside and signal back."

Elise held on to his shirt sleeve. "Peter, are you sure?"

"Sure, I'm sure. I'll keep an eye out. The clouds have made it pretty dark. Don't you think, Captain? They're signaling right now."

Even though the captain was in pain, he did his best to keep control of the situation. "Watch for anyone on the beach," he instructed Peter. It obviously was an effort to keep his eyes open, and he leaned heavily on the pastor. "Make sure it's all clear before you call in the boat. Flash back once at the cottage here when it's safe to come. It's important to make sure the Germans have passed by. Understand?"

"I understand." Peter gulped, knowing everyone was depending on him. He slipped out the door and crept along the dunes, closer to the beach. *Mikkel did say there aren't any mines along this part of the beach, didn't he?* Peter shuddered to think of stepping on one. But it was true, there wasn't any barbed wire along this section of sand. It looked safe enough.

Still overcast, the moon was in hiding. Peter glanced nervously down the beach, looking for anything that would move. All he saw was the white foam of breakers as waves crashed on the beach. Farther down the beach, he could make out the Bluewater Hook light, a friendly-looking flash every few seconds. He took a deep breath of the salt air. All clear, so far.

The other way looked much the same, beach disappearing into darkness. His eyes were used to it, but he still couldn't see anything. Too dark. He wished he could use his flashlight to sweep down the beach, but that would have been a dumb idea. Still, something made him pause a moment before he got ready to flash back the "all clear" signal. It was almost as if he smelled something different in the air, and he looked back to his right, up the beach. *Is someone there?*

The two soldiers and their dog almost walked right over Peter as he lay in the sand; he heard them before he saw them. They were chatting, and one must have told a joke, because the other laughed and slapped his companion on the back. Peter couldn't make out what they were saying. He just buried his face in the sand and tried to disappear. Now he was glad it was so dark, but would they step on him?

Peter could barely breathe. With his free hand, he carved out a small hole under his face. *What if the soldiers look out at the ocean and see a light flash?* There was nothing he could do but bury his face and pray. It seemed much more natural now—the praying—as if he were talking to someone he knew. But then, he *did* know better who he was praying to, now.

Peter lost track of how long he lay in the sand. Ten minutes, a little longer. Mikkel must have returned by then, and they were probably going to come out after him if he didn't do something soon. The soldiers had disappeared again into the darkness, not seeming to care about making noise. One kept telling jokes or something, and the other kept laughing. Even in the distance, Peter could still hear the laugh above the soft sound of the waves on the beach. *They must be far enough away by now,* he thought. But a strong grip on his shoulders made him freeze in terror.

"Shh," warned a still voice from behind. Peter spun around in the darkness, not sure what he would do if he came face-to-face with a German soldier.

"What are you doing out here?" asked the voice. It was Mikkel. Peter slumped back in the sand, his heart still pounding.

"Mikkel! I thought—"

"Sorry, Peter. I didn't mean to scare you like that. Your sister was worried you were taking so long. I just got back. What were you doing?"

"I was hiding. The Germans came by on the beach, and I was coming out here to signal to the boat. We saw a blinking light out there. And they almost walked right over me!" Peter stood up and brushed the sand off his clothes.

"Dog, too?" Mikkel sounded worried.

"Yeah, they had a dog."

"Okay," said Mikkel, taking charge. "That patrol was a little late, and the boat a little early, but it's probably just as well. At least now we know where they are. Did you signal back?"

"I didn't even get the chance to."

"That's all right." Mikkel dusted the sand off his knees. "If the patrol passed this way five minutes ago, they should be pretty far down the beach by now. Let's hurry before they come back. Go ahead and give the boat the 'C' signal."

Peter tried to recall exactly where he had seen the flashes of light. He pointed his light in that direction and moved the switch. A long flash, a short flash, then another long and short. He waited. Off in the darkness, a moment later, the same signal repeated back at him. *They saw!*

"Good," said Mikkel, sounding relieved. "Now let's hurry and get everybody back out here, before the Germans come back."

They trotted back to the cottage one more time, and Elise opened it a crack when Peter knocked quietly.

"What took you so long?" she asked.

"He can explain later," answered Mikkel. "German patrols." He turned to the pastor, his family, and the British flyer, shadows around the door. "We're off, then. Let's wait out by the beach. Peter and Elise, you stay here until I get back."

There were handshakes all around, and Pastor Kai gave Peter a bone-crushing hug. Then Peter remembered.

"Pastor Kai, there's one thing I have to tell you before you go." In the darkness, he could just make out the pastor's face. "And you, too, Jakob." Peter bent down to face the little boy. "Remember when you asked me in the sheep house the other day if I knew Jesus?"

Jakob nodded, still holding his mother. "I remember."

"Maybe you remember that I didn't answer you, too. But my sister asked me the same thing, and my uncle—I mean my other uncle back home in Helsingor; he asked me once, too. And you know what, Jakob?"

"What?"

"I finally decided to follow Jesus. Really!"

Even in the darkness, Peter thought he saw the little boy's face light up.

"See, Daddy?" Jakob looked up at Pastor Kai, excited. "I told you Peter would, I told you he would. We just had to keep praying!"

Pastor Kai put his arms around Peter in another bear hug, and Peter felt warm, all over.

"We were praying for you, Peter," said the pastor. "Jakob was, especially. And when a little boy prays, things happen, you know."

Peter knew just what the pastor meant. It felt like a welcome home, a feeling he'd never quite known before.

"I hate to break up the party," interrupted Mikkel, "but you're going to miss your boat if we don't get out to the beach. Those Brits don't like to wait around, especially with guards out walking every hour."

"Yes, of course," replied the pastor, sounding excited and very tired. Then Elise gave him a hug, and even Mrs. Steffensen and Jakob got in on the goodbyes.

"We'll be back soon," Mrs. Steffensen assured Elise, "as soon as all this is over. You be sure to tell your Aunt Hanne. We'll be back soon." She was crying, and it made Peter and Elise cry, too. Finally, Peter had to turn away.

The captain leaned against the doorway, then straightened and turned to Elise and Peter before he left. "I shall always be grateful to you for your help," Captain Whitbread told them in his shaky voice. "And thank you for the Danish lessons, Elise. Whenever I eat bread, I'll remember your awful language." He chuckled, then stiffened. "Your Uncle Harald will continue to be in my prayers as well. I'm so sorry about that."

"Come on," urged Mikkel. "Peter, I'll be back in a half hour, maybe an hour. Depends on how fast the boat comes. Keep the light out. When I get back, we'll just sleep here in the cabin, and go home tomorrow morning. Okay?"

"We'll be right here," promised Peter, wiping his nose with a sleeve. Then all he heard was the sound of breakers on the beach, and the others were gone.

12

Narrow Escape

The waiting was the worst part, Peter thought as he and Elise sat in the darkness of the beach house. All they heard was the almost musical rhythm of the waves, and Peter strained his ears to hear more. A dog barking, perhaps, or the soldier's coarse laugh. But there was only the crashing, a gentle thunder of ocean, and a hiss as each wave slipped back. Usually he loved the sound, but not tonight.

"You think they're gone yet?" Peter whispered to his sister, afraid to raise his voice. "It's been at least a half hour."

"Ten minutes," replied Elise. "It's only been ten minutes."

"Ten? Are you sure?"

"I'm sure." She held up her wristwatch to the crack in the window, but only she could make it out. "The boat should have been there by now, and—"

"And then they're on their way to England." Peter finished her sentence. "So where's Mikkel?"

Almost in answer to his question, Peter heard the door rattle as someone tried the doorknob.

"Just a minute," croaked Peter, and he jumped up to undo the latch. But before he could cross the room, the door crashed open, and Peter stared straight into a bright flashlight.

"Hey!" yelped Peter in surprise.

Peter was interrupted by a deep-throated growl as a soldier with a rifle stormed into the room. The dark shadow of a guard dog followed close behind.

"Down on the floor," the man yelled in German. "Niederlegen! Get down on the floor!" Framed in the doorway, Peter could make out a rifle pointed straight at him, for the second time in the same day. It wasn't any less horrifying this time, either. He looked over at Elise, who had been sitting on a chair by the only table in the room.

"Hören Sie? Do you hear?" The man yelled again, waving the rifle. Peter was sure he could probably be heard all the way down on the beach, the way he was shouting. Maybe even back on the farm. He and Elise fell to the floor and lay there, face down, trembling. *What are they going to do now?* thought Peter. *What if Mikkel comes back?*

The soldier with the dog searched the cottage, which took only a minute.

"Empty," he told the first soldier. "Looks like it's been that way for a while."

At that, the first one laughed, the way Peter had heard him do out on the beach.

"So, Dietrich, just a couple of kids, eh?" He poked at Peter's ribs with the tip of his boot, but not hard enough to hurt. "Get up, boy."

Peter and Elise got up and stood awkwardly in the middle of the room. Huddled together, they both crossed their arms and waited to see what the soldiers would do next. The dog sniffed at them at first, then seemed more interested in getting back outside. The second soldier kept him tightly leashed, though. Soldier Number One slung his rifle more casually around his shoulder, apparently convinced that Peter and Elise were no threat.

By the light of their flashlights, Peter could only tell that the first soldier was a little older, and the second soldier—the one who held the dog—must have been pretty young. Peter was glad at least that neither looked like the German who had stopped him and the pastor on the road. That, he knew, would have been a disaster.

"What are you two doing here?" asked the older soldier. Peter was afraid to look, but he saw the gray-green uniform and the shiny boots. He understood the words when the man repeated his question in half-Danish, a little slower. "Where do you live?"

Elise found her tongue first, while Peter couldn't even think. She did her best to mix in German words she knew.

"We were out for a bike trip," she squeaked. "We're staying with our aunt and uncle. Farm near Ho."

True. Shivering, Peter hoped they could just be done with the questions and get out of here before Mikkel came walking back in through the door. He nodded in agreement.

"Yes, yes, and it looks like you two found a mud puddle as well," replied the soldier. "But what were you doing here on the beach?" The man's voice had softened some since he came bursting through the door. "This isn't a place for children in the middle of the night."

"Excuse me?" Peter could tell his sister was doing her best to look calm. "We . . . we didn't know quite how far it was. It got late and . . . um . . . we decided to stay here for a few hours, until morning. Nobody lives here."

All true, thought Peter.

"You say your aunt and uncle live in Ho?" asked the soldier, lowering his rifle. "I think they would be worried that you haven't returned home." He straightened up from where he had leaned against the door. "But you were right not to travel alone after dark. You will come with us. Bring your bicycles." Unsure that they had understood, he steered his rifle like a set of bicycle handlebars and waved for them to follow.

There was no other option. Peter and Elise dug their bikes out of the bushes, and they followed the first soldier. The man with the dog followed close behind. Peter didn't know where they were being taken, but at least they were getting away from the cottage. Mikkel would come back to find them gone. Peter looked off toward the beach, and he thought he saw a dark shadow duck behind a dune.

The four of them hurried back out to the main road, then headed to the right, toward Oksby and away from the Ringsted farm. Finally Peter found the courage to say something.

"Excuse me," he said, "but where are you taking us?" He used the German word for "where," hoping the soldiers would understand.

The soldier stopped, and Peter saw the man's face for the first time in the light from the flashlight behind him. He was about their father's age, but shorter and stockier. He managed a shadow of a grin, then turned serious again.

"I have two teenage sons back home in Hamburg," he said before he turned back again. "Teenagers." The man grinned and pointed at Elise and Peter. "Your age, a little older. Almost old enough to serve the Fatherland. But still kids." He paused. "We're taking you home. Home." Then he pointed up the road. "Our truck is right up here."

Peter understood most of what the man had said; Elise helped to fill in the blanks. Peter thought how strange this was turning out to be. The men they were hiding from, their enemies, were giving them a lift home to the farm.

As they neared the beach town of Oksby, Peter saw where Mikkel had parked the bus, and he noticed the soldier looking at it as they walked by.

"Those people need to leave their bus in the garage, where it belongs," mumbled the first soldier.

Five more minutes of walking brought them to the outskirts of the town and to a small farm building with German trucks and vehicles parked around it. It was German headquarters, and Peter prayed the soldiers wouldn't make them go inside.

"Wait here," said the older man, holding up his hand. He disappeared into the building, a small brick house with a tile roof. Someone had lived there, before the war, before the Germans had come to take over the farm. Light spilled out from the open front door, and Peter heard voices inside. When the man returned, he motioned them into the back of a small gray truck. The young man and the dog hopped up beside them, and Peter backed away as far as he could from the animal.

"Ho?" asked the younger man. That was about the limit of his Danish, and Peter was in no mood to work on his German just then. He nodded, and hoped the soldier wouldn't try to carry on a conversation. Peter looked over at Elise. She was sitting behind her bicycle with her eyes closed. Sleeping or praying, Peter wasn't sure which.

"So where is the farm?" asked the older man, who was driving. He glanced back briefly through a small opening in the back of his cab. Without opening her eyes, Elise called back over the noise of the truck.

"Just outside of Ho. Turn right, and it's the last farm before you get to the bay."

The man nodded, and steered back toward the Ringsted farm. In the darkness, Peter tried to keep his bicycle from bouncing around too much, and the fumes and smoke nearly made him sick. Still, he was glad to be getting back to the Ringsted farm—even if it was in the back of a German army truck.

A while later the driver called back again. "Close?"

Peter tried to look up through the window at the dark road. He recognized a mailbox.

"Right up ahead," said Peter, pointing. But as soon as the words were out, he wondered. Would this man question them when he found out where they really lived? The farm where Uncle Harald lived? Surely the soldier would know.

But whether the man knew anything or not, he just kept driving. The truck lurched to a halt, and both Peter and Elise stood up with their bikes to get out. A minute later, they were down on the road, and the man was back in the truck. He leaned out his window.

"Now stay away from the beach, eh?" He waved his finger at them, and Peter could see the man outlined in the dim light of the cab. "You could have stepped on a mine, or run into someone else, not me."

Peter couldn't say anything. He couldn't bring himself to say thank you to this man, the man with the two teenage sons. Men with the same uniform held his two uncles prisoner. Men with this uniform had pointed guns and captured people he knew. Maybe not this man, but men with the same uniform. No, Peter couldn't say thank you, so he just nodded, and the truck disappeared in the darkness to the sound of grinding gears.

Peter and Elise stood at the end of the Ringsted driveway for a long minute, both quiet, each in their own thoughts. It started to rain again.

"Come on." Elise pulled Peter by the sleeve. She started to wheel her bicycle down the gravel path. "Let's get back to the house."

An animal came running out to greet them, and Peter knew almost without looking who it was. Milky Way! The orphan sheep nuzzled his friend, and Peter almost fell over from exhaustion.

"Sorry, little guy," Peter whispered as he reached down and scratched the lamb's nose. "No bottle for you right now."

BEYOND THE RIVER

Mikkel came biking home the next day, but he didn't want to talk about what had happened. Still, Kurt pestered him after breakfast, like a dog in a sheep pen.

"Come on, Mikkel, can't you at least tell us that everyone got away safe? Marianne and I waited in Oksby for almost two hours, and nobody ever showed!"

"I know, Kurt." Mikkel's eyes were only half open, and he picked at the last bite of bread on his plate. Peter wondered if he had slept at all. "I appreciate what you did. Everyone got away fine."

"That's it?" Kurt wasn't going to let it drop so easily. "Peter and Elise got a ride home with a German soldier, in a German truck, and you get home this morning, and that's it?"

Aunt Hanne slammed her palm down on the table, her eyes flashing. "That's it, and that's all there will be," she declared, her voice trembling. "We will hear no more about this rescue business, about sneaking around at night, about airplanes, about

British flyers, or submarines, or about anything like that. Does everyone understand? Your father is still not home, and, and . . ."

With that she pushed her chair out from the table and rushed from the room. Everyone sat stone still, and Peter tried to look at Mikkel and Kurt without turning his head.

"See what you did?" Marianne gave her brothers a hard look.

Kurt threw up his hands. "What did I say?"

"You had to keep pushing at it, didn't you, Kurt?" Mikkel glared at his younger brother. "Mom was right. You just need to back off the whole thing."

Kurt's eyes flashed. "Well, then, how about you, Mr. Underground? She was talking to you, too!"

"Grow up," snapped Mikkel. "She didn't mean me. You know that as well as I do. Wait until Dad gets home."

That was too much for Marianne, and she quickly followed her mother out of the kitchen—crying. Peter had no stomach for an argument, either, so he looked over at Elise and signaled at her with a jerk of his head. They left the room together, while Kurt and Mikkel were still sniping at each other. Peter wasn't even sure the brothers had noticed everyone leaving.

———

And that was the way it continued for the next few days. Kurt and Mikkel would argue, but not in front of their mother. With Uncle Harald gone, everyone had to do double chores. Wilhelm and Johann returned from their leave late Sunday night but left early the next morning to return to their work at the radar station. Peter and Elise helped as much as they could, feeding horses, cleaning, collecting eggs, even doing wash. There was always something else to do, it seemed, and Peter didn't mind that part. *If I could just figure out a way to keep Mikkel and Kurt from arguing,* he thought, *things would be so much easier.*

But Uncle Harald had still not come home, and Aunt Hanne

grew more and more weary each day. The spark that Peter had always noticed in her eyes had fizzled. Some mornings she didn't even get out of bed; other times she retired early and closed the door behind her. She smiled at them from her bed Wednesday morning, the fifth morning after the night of the escape. Peter had never seen his aunt look so sickly and frail.

"I hear that the trains are running again," she said, pulling the covers up to her chin. "Is that right?" She looked as if she was trying hard to put on her best face.

Peter looked at her, wondering. He hadn't heard anything. If it was true, that meant they would have to go home. Even though things had not been happy at the Ringsted farm the last week, Peter felt that they were helping somehow.

"That's what Mikkel said," continued Aunt Hanne.

Marianne was out in the kitchen, making noise at the stove. "Did you want something to eat this morning, Mom?" she yelled.

Aunt Hanne was staring at a wall hanging, another piece of fine needlepoint her mother had made. The morning sunlight played on the wall, and she watched a flicker of a shadow as a robin flew past the window outside. Then she looked over at Elise, who had come quietly into the room with Peter.

"I'm sorry," apologized Aunt Hanne. "What did you say?"

"Oh, it wasn't me. Marianne just wanted to know if you want anything to eat. You ... you haven't been eating very much, Aunt Hanne."

"No, maybe I haven't." Her voice trailed off. Peter thought he could almost see a gray rain cloud hovering over her bed. He had really never seen anyone so depressed before, and it scared him.

No one said anything for a few moments, while Peter stared out the window and stewed about the week. If they were going to have to go back home soon, this was not the way he wanted to leave. Not while everyone was either captured by the Germans, depressed, or crabby. He gave the curtain a toss and turned around.

"That's it, Aunt Hanne," announced Peter, surprising himself with his own voice. "I'm going to see what's going on. I can't stand not knowing."

"What are you talking about?" asked Elise. She nearly dropped the tray of food she was carrying in for her aunt.

"I'm talking about Uncle Harald." Peter knew what he was going to say now. "I don't know how, but I'm going to find out, that's all. Mikkel doesn't know. We don't know. Everybody's going crazy. So I'm going to find out. That's what I'm talking about." Peter felt angry, not at his sister, but at the whole crazy situation. "And when I find out about Uncle Harald, and we get back home, I'm going to find out about Uncle Morten, too."

"Peter," cautioned Elise, setting down the tray. "You can't just walk up to the next German soldier you see."

"I know that." Now the plan in his head made perfect sense. "I'm going to go to Oksby, to that headquarters building where they took us after finding us in the beach house, and I'm going to find out. I'm just going to go. We've prayed and prayed about this, and I think—"

"You've got to be kidding, Peter," his sister protested again.

"I'm not kidding," he insisted. Peter looked at his aunt, who was now staring at him with her mouth gaping open, listening to every word.

"Look, Aunt Hanne." Peter stepped over to the bed. "Don't you remember you told me about Joshua? He stood up to everybody, right? Didn't he say something like, 'I don't know what you're going to do, but, but . . .'" Peter knew what he wanted to say, but it wasn't coming out quite the way he wanted. He didn't want to suggest that they take on the entire German army. He just wanted to do something for Uncle Harald besides sit in the house under a dark cloud.

"But as for me and my house," quoted Aunt Hanne, "we will serve the Lord."

Aunt Hanne had been propped up in her bed, wrapped in her large robe. Suddenly she threw back her covers, swung out her feet, and stood up. Something inside her had woken up.

"Your brother is right, Elise," announced Aunt Hanne, slowly at first. She looked as if she was building up a steam to match Peter's. "This is crazy. Absolutely crazy. But what is really crazy is me sitting here in bed, crying and feeling sorry for myself."

"Mom?" Marianne poked her head into the bedroom. "Did you want some more eggs?"

"No!" Aunt Hanne almost shouted, and Marianne backed up, startled.

"Peter is not going to Oksby alone," declared Aunt Hanne. "He is coming with me. And if anyone else wants to come along, that's fine, too. We are going to march right up to those Germans and find out what they have done with my husband." She clapped Peter on the back and smiled for the first time in days. "I don't know why we didn't do this before, Peter. Now, let me get dressed, and I'll be right out."

Peter couldn't help feeling as if he were marching in a military parade, only there were no flags flying out front. But flags or no, Aunt Hanne led the way out of the house, followed by Peter and Elise, then Marianne and Kurt. Mikkel was out repairing another fence.

Poor Kurt, thought Peter, as they marched out the front door. *He has no idea what got into his mother.* Kurt had just been swept along with the parade as he came back from doing his own chores.

"What's going on?" whispered Kurt. His face was a question mark.

Peter hurriedly filled him in as they pulled their bicycles from the barn.

"So what do we do when we get there, Mom?" asked Kurt.

"I'm not exactly sure," replied his mother. "We'll think of that on the way. Right now, I just know we're going to go."

They pedaled in the same parade order all the way to the outskirts of Oksby, forty-five minutes away, following the same route Peter and Elise had taken when they were chasing the pastor. They passed the beach road that led down to the summer cottage by the sea, and Peter peeked back at Elise. She recognized the road, too.

When they all reached the small house that was German headquarters, Peter didn't need to point it out to his aunt. Several German army trucks and a car with red Nazi flags on the fenders were parked out in front. It looked like the same car that had gone through the roadblock with them the time they were traveling with the pastor, the time he was hiding the radio.

Taking a deep breath, Aunt Hanne stopped her bike, got off, and carefully leaned it against the outside wall by the front door.

"Come on," she said to her small army. "We're going to find out what happened to your father."

Inside, what had been a sitting room had been turned into the Nazis' main office. Voices came from several rooms where officers were meeting. A young clerk sitting at a desk looked up in surprise at the woman who now confronted him. The kids lined up behind Aunt Hanne. She spoke before the young clerk in uniform could open his mouth.

"I'm Hanne Ringsted, and I've come to find out what's become of my husband. You took him away for questioning nearly a week ago, and he's not been released yet."

She crossed her arms and stood her ground, waiting for an answer.

The young man looked at her blankly, studied all the young people behind her, and held up his finger.

"One moment," he said in German. "Sprechen Sie Deutsch? Do you speak German?"

"No," Aunt Hanne answered in Danish, showing her teeth like a watchdog. "You're going to have to understand what I'm saying in Danish."

The clerk just shook his head, pushed out his chair, and disappeared down the hall. Peter peeked around the corner, and he could see the young man talking with a gray-uniformed officer, motioning out at them and shrugging. A few minutes later, the gray-haired officer—an older man of about sixty—followed the clerk out to the front room. It was not a man they had seen before, and Peter breathed a quiet sigh of relief.

"I understand you're inquiring about your husband," he addressed Aunt Hanne, studying the crowd in his office. He spoke passable Danish, though Peter thought it sounded more like German than anything else.

"That's right," replied Aunt Hanne. "Is he here? The name is Harald Ringsted."

"Yes, yes, I know who you're talking about." The man nodded impatiently. "Sheep farmer, correct? He was here." He looked down at some papers on the desk and shuffled through a notepad.

"Was?"

"Yes. When he refused to cooperate with our investigation here, he was transferred to another facility."

Aunt Hanne looked hopeful. "So is he all right? Where did they take him? When will he be released?"

By that time the officer was through with his side of the conversation, and he started to slip back into German.

"Ja, ja, Frau, eh, Rinkstedt." He waved his hand to dismiss Aunt Hanne and started to turn around. "He's been taken to Vestre Prison, but he will be released as soon as he cooperates with us. Unless, of course, it is found that he is guilty of other crimes. You are dismissed." Then the man turned to the young clerk. "Corporal, show these people out." Then he disappeared down the hall.

There was no chance to say anything else. When they were back on their bikes and heading home again, Peter looked over at his aunt. She looked far away, thinking.

"Mom, what time is it?" asked Kurt.

Aunt Hanne looked at her small wristwatch. "Ten, Kurt. It's ten o'clock." She answered her son, but her voice sounded far away.

"At least we found out he's okay," said Peter. He wasn't sure if that was the best thing to say at the time.

Aunt Hanne looked over at her nephew and half smiled. "Yes, you're right. Now all we can do is keep praying."

Peter and Elise had been praying for Uncle Harald, but just then something told Peter that it was time to pray again. *Strange,* he wondered. *It's almost like an alarm clock went off inside.* Peter stopped his bike, and everyone looked back.

"Aunt Hanne," Peter called.

"Are you all right?" asked his aunt, putting on her brakes.

"I'm fine," he answered. "But we need to pray right now for Uncle Harald. I'm not sure why, but we just need to pray now."

Aunt Hanne gave him a puzzled look, but only for a moment. She pulled her bike back around, followed by Marianne and Kurt. Elise did the same.

"That's fine, Peter." Aunt Hanne looked briefly up and down the country road for any approaching traffic. They were the only ones on the road just then. "Would you like to pray for us?"

Peter nodded, and everyone in the small group bowed their heads.

"Dear God," Peter began, not sure of his next words. He took a deep breath. "Please, would you please take care of Uncle Harald. Please get him out of prison. And . . . and I pray for the soldiers. I don't know why, but I just do. In Jesus' name, amen."

As they pedaled back down the road, Peter still wasn't sure where the prayer had come from, or why he had thought it was so important to stop just then and there. But thinking about it gave him an expectant feeling, a little bit like the day before Christmas.

Milky Way was waiting for them by the front door when they made it back to the farm, so Peter went in to find him his bottle. After feeding him, the kids went to find Mikkel, with the lamb following after them. Or rather, it followed Peter, nipping at his heels. They found Mikkel at the edge of the woods, lowering a fence post into a hole he had just dug.

"So where have you all been?" Mikkel grunted as he lowered his post into place. "I went back to the house, and everyone was gone."

"We rode out to Oksby to find out if the Germans could tell us when Dad was coming home," replied Kurt matter-of-factly. Peter hoped they wouldn't start fighting again.

Mikkel's jaw dropped open, then he snapped it shut. Peter thought his cousin looked like Aunt Hanne when he did that. "You did what?" Mikkel let go of his post and looked at the four of them. "Are you kidding? Whose idea was that?"

Everyone looked at Peter, who just shrugged.

"Mom's idea, mostly," admitted Marianne. "She was great, talking to this German officer. But Dad wasn't there."

"So where is he?" Mikkel wanted to know. "Nobody I've talked to can tell me anything."

"Copenhagen," announced Kurt. "They've taken him to the city. Vestre Prison."

They were quiet for a minute, waiting to hear what else Mikkel would say.

"How did you figure where Vestre Prison was?" Mikkel asked his brother.

"I'm not stupid," countered Kurt. "Not like—"

"Okay, okay, I've heard it," interrupted Mikkel. He slammed the post down into its hole and grunted. "Now I could use some help to finish this fence. How about it?"

Peter thought for a minute, and then he had an idea.

"Nope," he replied firmly. Then he crossed his arms and planted his feet. "I'm not going to help until you two stop your arguing." Peter kept his arms crossed and tried to look firm. "Well?"

"Who says we've been arguing?" asked Kurt. That only caused Marianne to give him a shove.

"Oh, come on," she said. "Peter's right. That's all we've been hearing from you two for the past few days. You need to shake hands and apologize."

"Yeah," agreed Peter, keeping his arms crossed. "Shake hands, and let's all see it."

Mikkel looked at his brother and started to grin. "Well," he admitted. "What if I'm not sorry?"

"Mikkel!" Kurt picked up a dirt clod to throw at his brother. "You've just been a total boss since Dad—since Dad left."

"Yeah? And you've been a total brat."

This time Peter stepped between the warring brothers. "Anything else?" Peter looked from cousin to cousin.

"I do need the help," admitted Mikkel. "So if that's the only way we're going to get it from Peter, we better shake hands, Kurt."

"Hmm." Kurt scratched his chin. "Does this mean we can't ever fight again?"

Mikkel looked over at Peter and tried to cork his smile. "What do you say, Peter? How long?"

"At least a week of no arguments," Peter decided, still thinking. "No, a month. One month of no arguing. Even after Elise and I go back home. Deal?"

Mikkel stuck out his hand past Peter, and Kurt hesitated before taking it. Peter clamped the two hands together and Elise clapped.

"There!" said Mikkel, still pumping his brother's hand with a big, playful motion. Neither one would let go first. "Now hand that man a shovel, Marianne!" He pointed to Peter and a pile of tools.

They worked on the fence the rest of that morning, with Peter and Kurt taking turns digging holes, Marianne holding wire, and Elise hammering nails. Once in a while, they all had to chase sheep (especially Milky Way) away from the parts they were working on. Around one o'clock, Aunt Hanne came out to the field with rye-bread sandwiches, apples, and a jug of water for lunch.

"It's the least I can do for such hard workers," said Aunt Hanne cheerfully. Since they had ridden to Oksby, she seemed more like herself again. Still worried, but more like herself. She looked at her sons for a moment. Kurt was holding a roll of wire for Mikkel, who was attaching it to the post.

"No arguments today?" she asked her sons.

The boys looked at each other, and Kurt started to giggle.

"I forgot what we were arguing about," mumbled Mikkel, bending down.

Everyone stopped working in the late afternoon, the way they always did when their father was home and they used to hear the BBC broadcast. Everyone filed into the house, washed up their arms and faces, and took their places at the kitchen table. Uncle Harald's place was empty, of course, and Aunt Hanne glanced over as she prayed before the meal. They started without Johann and Wilhelm, who were unusually late.

Peter looked over at Kurt and Marianne, who were picking at their food. The adventure of marching to the German headquarters that morning had lifted their spirits for a while, but when they got home, their father was still not there. Peter thought again about leaving on the train in the morning, leaving without knowing what had become of his uncle.

"I wonder who's going to be the new pastor, now that Pastor Kai and his family are gone?" asked Marianne. She swirled the water in her glass as she said it.

"That's right." Aunt Hanne sliced another piece of bread. "I hadn't even thought of that, but the bishop is going to have to send someone else. Perhaps the pastor from Vejle will fill in for a few weeks, until they can find someone."

Kurt sighed. "It's not going to be the same. Everybody's gone. And now Peter and Elise have to go, too."

Mikkel had his elbow on the table and his head in his hand, but his mother didn't even scold him. He was looking out the window when he suddenly dropped his fork on the floor and rushed to the door.

"Mikkel!" said his mother. "Whatever are you doing? Are the two German boys finally here?"

Mikkel didn't say anything; he just threw open the door.

"Dad!" everyone shouted at once and mobbed around Uncle Harald as he tried to get into his house. He started to laugh, and grabbed as many as he could.

"Let me get in, let me get in before you tackle me!" he told them. The kids backed off, leaving only Aunt Hanne clutching her husband, tears streaming down her face.

When Aunt Hanne finally let him go, Uncle Harald looked almost the same, Peter thought, only very tired and dirty. There were gray lines below his eyes, and his cheeks looked shallow. His hair was tousled and messy, too. And he had what looked like a nasty black eye. Finally he settled down in his favorite living room chair.

"Dad." Mikkel pulled up another chair, close to his father. "How did you get home? They told us you were taken to Copenhagen."

"That's where I was this morning," explained Uncle Harald. "Vestre Prison. I thought I was spending a long time there, from what they told me."

"So how—" asked Marianne.

"How am I here now?" he finished her question, shaking his head slightly. "I'm honestly still not sure. You help me figure it.

They called me in this morning, the way they did every day. And the clerk had a funny expression, as if he couldn't figure something out. All he says when I report there is that he's received notice that I'm to be released that morning, immediately. So I don't wait to ask any more questions. They push me out the door, and I get on the next train home. So here I am!" He finished his story with a sweep of his arm.

"What time?" asked Elise. She had that expression on her face, the one that told Peter she was thinking about something. The Brain was working.

"What time was I released?" Uncle Harald didn't quite follow.

"Yes. What time, exactly?"

"Oh, I'm not sure," answered Uncle Harald. "No, wait a minute. It was ten, I mean ten-fifteen." He chuckled. "I looked at the clock while I stood waiting for the clerk to figure out what was wrong with my papers. Or what was right with them, actually. He never did figure it out."

"Ten-fifteen!" announced Elise in her "ah-ha" voice. "Do you know what else was happening at exactly the same time?"

Peter thought back to the morning, riding to the German headquarters. . . .

Aunt Hanne smiled and took her husband's hand. "Dear," she explained, "we were riding our bicycles down the road just then when Peter made us all stop and pray for you. It had to be right then and there. He insisted. I thought it was just a little odd, but we all prayed for you and that you would somehow come home. And right then was the right time, it seems."

Uncle Harald just stared at his wife as the full meaning of what had happened sunk in, then a smile broke out on his face. Peter had to pinch himself to believe things were happening like this. The prayer this morning, Uncle Harald back home tonight.

"Oh, Peter, Elise," said Uncle Harald suddenly. "I have to tell you." His face was serious but excited. "About someone I saw in the prison in Copenhagen."

Peter didn't want to guess, but he had a feeling inside. He looked over at Elise, who shook her head.

"Morten. Your father's brother. They were leading him down the hall one day when I was being taken the opposite way. He saw me, I'm sure, because he looked at me for a second. But we couldn't say anything."

"Wow, really?" asked Peter. "How did he look?"

"Was he okay, could you tell?" added Elise.

Uncle Harald cleared his throat. "I have to tell you he didn't look real good—pretty skinny. But he was walking fine, and he almost smiled at me. Of course, I don't know him that well, and the last time I saw him was probably before the war—Christmas when you were little. But I remember that spark in his eyes. It was still there. He's holding out."

"Hey, Peter." Kurt put his hand on Peter's shoulder. "So maybe if we keep praying for him, the way we did for Dad. . . ."

Peter looked over at his cousin and smiled. That was Kurt. This time, though, Peter didn't mind. At the same time, he felt a mixture of relief and sadness at hearing the news about Uncle Morten, who had been captured by the Germans for his part in helping Jews escape. *At least Uncle Morten is still alive!* thought Peter. *There's a chance now.*

Uncle Harald looked straight at Peter, then at Elise. "I thought you'd want to know."

"That's great news, I think." Elise managed a shy smile.

"Yeah, Uncle Harald," agreed Peter. "It is good news."

"But, Dad." Mikkel sat down on the arm of the living room chair. "You have to tell us, maybe not now if you don't want to, but how did you make it through without telling them anything? Or did you?"

Uncle Harald laughed, and it seemed out of place. "It was simple, really." He looked at Kurt. "Whenever the Nazis asked me a question, I would give them my best Molbo expression, and think of you and your jokes." Uncle Harald showed them his blank face, and everyone laughed. The gloom of the dinner table was chased away.

"But they still hit you," said Aunt Hanne, with concern in her voice. She reached over to touch her husband's eye, and he pulled away.

"Careful," he warned. Then he smiled again. "I think I even had them wondering if I could remember my own name. Kind of like that Englander, eh? By the way, Mikkel, I assume he's made it back to England?"

"Yeah, he's gone, Dad." Mikkel pulled on his sock and looked down. "We'll tell you everything that happened, but it's a long story."

"I understand." Uncle Harald nodded, then he looked over at the wall clock and slapped his oldest son on the back. "So! Mikkel!" he boomed. "Why don't you turn up the radio? Isn't it time for the BBC?"

Mikkel beamed as he jumped to the radio and fiddled with the controls. "Sure, Dad, but if Johann and what's-his-name get back, we'll have to cut it off."

"They're late tonight, for the first time in a while," explained Aunt Hanne. "Maybe they stopped somewhere on the way—"

A crackle from the radio interrupted her, and then everyone heard the familiar tune announcing their broadcast. "This is the BBC from London," came the announcer, and the seven of them settled down to hear news from the war and from the world. His ears perked up when the announcer reached the part where they passed on special messages.

"Shh," said Mikkel. But everyone was already still. The announcer faded out for a moment.

"And we'd like to pass along greetings to Dagmar from the pilot and the preacher," said the announcer.

"Hey!" said Peter, straining to hear.

"They want to thank those who helped them along the way," continued the radio voice. "The preacher also wants to say to his special friend, welcome to the family, and he's glad you made it from beyond the river. . . ."

Elise turned to Peter with a full smile. "That was for you!" she told him.

Peter just nodded.

"From beyond the river?" asked Kurt. "What was that supposed to mean?" As usual, he was the last one to figure things out. Peter could tell Aunt Hanne knew what it meant, though, because she glanced up at the wall hanging, the one Peter's grandmother had stitched but not quite finished. Then she winked at Peter and Elise and got up from her chair. She walked over to the wall, reached up, and gently lifted the hanging off its hook. She handed it to Peter.

"This is for you," she told him. "It will help you remember the verse, and what it means to us."

Peter managed a surprised "thank you." He stared at the cross-stitch in his hands and wondered if he should say anything else. Like Mikkel had said, it was a long story. And like the cross-stitch, he knew that it wasn't finished yet.